Demon

The smell of raw meat lingered

By Anthony Reif

Living Beyond Life, LLC

DEDICATION

This book is dedicated to everyone who has gone through
the same situations that my character does in this book.
I am sorry.
I am all too familiar with the pain you are going through.
It's weird to think this is the way it has to be, like we are not in
control of our own lives, but sometimes that is the reality of it.
Remember, you are never alone, you just have to seek help.

CONTENTS

Chapter 1
Raising the Dead

I always thought of myself as a good Christian. I was brought up 'right' by my parents, who were devout Catholics. I feel like that was an excuse to be harder on me than necessary. Like it gave them permission. It is hard to see things from another perspective when you are young.

How was I supposed to know my life would turn out this way? I can still see her eyes glowing red, just a few feet in front of me. The unassuming blue faded when she turned serious. I would wonder if she was going to kiss me or kill me. It used to feel so good. I'm getting ahead of myself. I am not sure if I should talk very much more about my own past before I continue to the important stuff. Meeting her, I mean. That's what the story is about. A girl, but not just any girl, as you may have realized. She proved to me that evil exists, but with that, good has to exist as well. Sometimes we invite it into our world. It is a choice that we make, whether conscious or not.

There isn't very much to say about my life. I did everything I was supposed to. I went to college and got a bachelor's degree. I went to church with my family, even though it made me nauseous most of the time.

Something about being crammed in this little uncomfortable wooden booth surrounded by people you don't know, was just not that pleasant. Especially, when you are a tiny child. My brother even passed out once. Freaked everyone out. I felt the same way most of the

1

time, but managed to stay conscious. I guess that is one way of getting out of going to church.

I don't know if there really is any merit in that kind of organized religion or not, but as a kid it didn't make very much sense. I even wanted to be a priest when I was younger. He got to stand up there without people touching him. He had so much space to move around, and was orchestrating the whole thing. I wanted to be in control. That's what they tell you when you are young. One day you will be in control. Not in those words, per say. It's more: you can be and do whatever you want, but when that time comes you end up being a waiter, saving what you are passionate about for your spare time. Try to do what you love, but also make enough money to survive.

They call them servers now. Waiters and waitresses. They are of a certain caliber. Always seemingly lost people. The ones who know what they are doing get out of it right away for something else. We are all lost souls wandering about the world, or the workplace.

People are either great or terrible at their jobs. In that industry, with that kind of potential, it is hard to be in between the two. Most of them are terrible. Sometimes the good ones look terrible. It all comes down to each individual dining with you that night. Say one thing goes wrong, suddenly you are bad at your job and it's your fault. Then you get a review online that says you deserve to be out on the street. That's what being the front man buys you. Everyone thinks they are the only one in the restaurant. The only one in the world. They think their feelings ride on you, instead of themselves. It's just another job. I don't know. I thought things were going well until they hired more people and cut back my hours. It's not that they didn't like me, even though they never said they did. They just didn't have enough shifts and decided it was okay to favor the new people over the better old ones. To be fair, they said. They later found out that people who have been working there for years just so happen to be better. What a surprise. That's beside the point, the reason I'm talking about this is that it led me to have to get a second job, and that's where I first met her.

Unsuspecting. I started this new job and felt the relief of being somewhere new for once. New people. New place. No responsibility. Only two days a week. Some sort of new freedom. I liked the people I worked with. There were so many people coming and going each shift. Over one hundred and fifty customers every day eating their meals and then leaving. That and the staff. It changed almost as often. Except for a select few who could deal with working there. I could. Most of the time. I guess I still do. It's just different now. She said it would be. I don't agree. The logic was faulty. Too late is too late. There is no going back. I feel like I should quit. Get her out of my life. Maybe. I loved every second of it.

Things went normally the first few months before she grew attached to me. I was on top of the world. Loving everyone. I did my best to become love, to radiate warmth and acceptance for everyone, knowing that there was nothing these people had to offer me. It is better to spread love because love is not a limited resource. It grows with use. You only have more and more, as you use it, and more comes back to you. So I was serving there, and being told how much everyone loved me. It was a new experience for me. My other job would never be so giving in compliments.

I missed one day for a religious holiday and when I turned my phone back on, there were texts about how they missed me. Wow. I had never had that happen at a restaurant, or any other job for that matter. I was certainly making an impact. Ah, about the religious festival. I have to talk about that at some point. When I got out of college I found that Eastern spirituality was more to my liking than Western. Much more loving and celebratory of the divine, whatever that may be. It has been working a lot better for me since, but it turns out there is much more to both than we encounter in normal life.

To be honest, I didn't even know who was texting me. There were too many people to enter and save their information in my phone, but there was a list of numbers that I could reference to see who it was. The first one is the big one. The others were servers and hosts, but they don't play much of a part in this story. The first one was the bartender, Jenny. I liked talking to her while I was working. A captive audience so to speak, but she would listen to my ramblings about whatever it was that I was thinking in the moment. She was good at her job. I noticed that right away.

Restaurants are all about how each person functions. The kitchen has to do it perfectly, as does the server, the host, the management, the bartender, and every other member of the staff, for everything to go well. One thing wrong, and it's a domino effect. Then people see angry people around them, and they get upset too. Energy is contagious. Pretty soon I'm left wanting to cry because one table got a steak that wasn't hot enough for them. And no tip.

It's worse when people who have 'worked in the industry' are rude. They should know better. You're serving three hundred people during one shift and they expect everything to be as fast and perfect as normal. Not going to happen. Try eating at home with your family on a holiday next time. I think people are at restaurants on the holidays because even their extended families don't want to be around them. Why do restaurants overbook? Money I guess. I told them they should just raise the price on those days and do less covers with higher quality service and food. They don't get it. They still want to serve an eight dollar hamburger that requires a perfect temperature, to three hundred people. It's not surprising that things go wrong. I am getting lost again. Not telling the story. Maybe I am avoiding it. It's hard for me to think about.

She's a demon. There. I spilled the beans. Ruined the big plot twist. So sue me. You can stop reading now. I hope you're taking my side on this. It's easy to follow attractive women. Especially if you are a little doggy male, tongue hanging out of his mouth, hoping for a treat. Fuck you. We all let instinct take over our senses. Men are animals. Accept it. You have to in order to live in this world, especially as a female. People are rarely sincere. Someone once said it is an endless cycle of people hurting each other, leading to everyone being closed off and self-serving. I can see how that would happen. I had been closed off for so long. "Heart closed indefinitely. No entry allowed." But at this point I had been practicing love. Love everyone. Accept the things you cannot change, change the things you cannot accept. Realize this is all impermanent, part of a dream, a fleeting moment, this too shall pass. Where is it now? Only in my mind. Where the accuracy is continually degrading. Things are never as they seem. Remember that. Before your heart gets broken. People care less about you than what you can provide for them. Whether it's social status, money, power, or even attention.

Chapter 2

Night, the First

When I walked in that day and saw her, I didn't think very much of it. Beside that she was attractive. I have a thing for tall girls. Better symmetry for the couple. Like attracts like. She had natural red hair, down to her shoulders. Pale white skin, that later I would find to be as soft as silk. The perfect figure, I had never dated someone whose body I liked up to this point. Some kind of fucked up relationship at least, I don't know if dating is the right word. It started off that way. Who can say. Later, she would be locked in an old wine refrigerator while I slept, wondering if she could get out. Right now, she was the most beautiful person in my life. Not that I was looking for it. Darling blue eyes always matching her outfit. I noticed. I told her so. I don't know how long it was that we had been flirting with each other. Eventually she started putting her arms around me while I sat at the bar folding napkins. It was then, I realized that maybe it wasn't just me that felt this way. I thought she was in a relationship. I met her boyfriend at the bar a few times. She always had dinner waiting for him. That was generous. Neither of them ever paid for it. He didn't even tip. I don't think I have seen anyone in a restaurant do that before. Especially on a regular basis. I respected that. "I don't even know who you are," she told me once. Funny. It is me who should have been saying that to her.

So it came down to it. I waited while she closed the restaurant and walked her to her car. But we didn't go to her car. We walked all around the block, talking about everything in our lives that was going on. When we got back to her car, I hugged her, but noticed that she wasn't expecting my head to go past hers. It was time for a kiss. I didn't care if she was in a relationship or not. Love is love, passion is passion, what is in the moment is meant to be. If it feels right, go with it. If you turn away what the universe provides, it will stop providing. So we kissed. A few times. Then she said goodnight and walked to her car. "It has been," I said, walking back to my apartment. Hmph. So she did like me. Like that. Interesting. I wasn't completely sure how I felt at that moment. I liked her too, but never expected anything to come from it. It had gone well.

The next night, I worked with her as well. When we went outside afterward, we didn't hold back. Maybe I did. No. I just wasn't so invested as she seemed to be. I was just enjoying the moment, not getting too worked up about it. Kissing each other against the side of the building. Feeling her soft skin, and caressing her hair. She was more rough than I was. Rain drops were falling on us from the sky, getting our clothes wet. The chill was cut through by the inner warmth of being close to her. It was beautiful. She agreed.

"Most people would think this is crazy," she said. She kept protesting. Like we couldn't do it. I told her that I was just in the moment, not the future, or anywhere else. Enjoying what we had. That is all I ever try to do. Enjoy the moment. Not what could be, good or bad, what is. The rain stopped and we were still pushing each other against the brick wall, first one, than the other. "Kiss me like you mean it," she kept telling me. It seemed that she had more invested at this point. I don't know. I was enjoying it, but it wasn't that important to me, no matter how beautiful it was in the moment. She kept thinking of all the reasons not to enjoy it. "You are really stuck in your head," I told her. It was sad in some way. Missing the best part of the moment. She was biting and sucking on my neck. It seemed very rough, but I didn't see any marks later when I looked in the mirror. I don't know how she did it.

"We have to go slow, you have to trust me," she said. I agreed. I didn't want to rush this. I doubt most girls have ever heard a guy say that truthfully. I said it. I even meant it. Last time I was in this situation, I knew it was one of those now or never sort of things, so I pressed upon it, and got what I wanted. This time was different. I really wanted to build something bigger, and that is what I did. It was three o'clock when we finished. We had been kissing for three hours. So called adults are missing out on the kissing business. It creates a deep bond and connection. So I walked home alone that night, shirt now dry from when the rain had been making it more fun. I slept like a rock. Blacked out so to speak, but felt good. I don't remember the last time I kissed someone like that.

I wouldn't be seeing her again until the next week. I only worked there two days after all. I was exhilarated. This could be the beginning of something big and unexpected. I felt connected to the universe again. Like I was part of a whole. At my first job, Chez Fe, I talked to my best friend, Zach, about it.

"You are of the same kind," I told him. Zach had red hair as well. He always referred to it like it was some sort of a pack.

"She's smart?" Zach asked.

"No," I replied. "She also has red hair. Natural."

"She's a ginger?"

"Yes. Very soft, smooth, pale skin, but yes, she is smart too. At least I think she is."

"Oh, so you think she's like us?" he asked me.

"Yes."

"That's great, I'm happy for you, buddy."

That was how the conversation went. Short and sweet. I wanted to share my excitement with someone who I knew I could count on in life. We were two of a kind, or three now.

Later during the week, Jenny texted me the same argument: that she was not sure if it could work out and that it would put stress on us at the workplace. I didn't care about that, and she should have known that. I told her that whatever she decided I would support. I didn't hear anything after that. The next time we worked together she was far more distant. No more touching. I could tell she still felt the same way when I looked at her eyes, but it hurt. It was already too late for me to turn back. It felt like a selfish thing she was doing. I had said it because it was the right thing to do. Not because I felt the same way. Only out of logic. Not following her heart. How could anyone live like that? I always thought I was the feelingless one. I tried my best to act normal, but everyone could tell I was disturbed. I was angry the whole day. Mad at everything. Then I drank some espresso to calm myself down. It helped. My mind was lighter. I tried to come to terms with it. I waited while she closed, and walked her to her car. A hug. I pulled away wishing our lips could embrace once again. Was that my job? She turned away from me quickly, possibly reading my mind. Not wanting to linger. My feelings never changed. As she sat in the driver seat, I saw the faraway look in her eyes, somewhere deep down. She wanted it too, but wouldn't let herself. Couldn't let herself. So I walked home alone again.

Chapter 3

I Wonder What She Looks Like Naked

Back to work. My regular job, Chez Fe. One more week before I would see her again. So what? What was there to see anymore? A loss? Something that could have been, if she had followed her heart? I spent a long time meditating on it. Trying to work through it. I hadn't expected it in the first place, and here I was having to recover from it. That seemed unfair. I was in such a good place before this. Seriously. I figured when she said she would hurt me that it was going to be far off in the future, not before anything even happened. "It's so weird, I don't know why, but when you are gone I miss you." That's what she had said to me. Like it wasn't okay to have these feelings for me.

I managed to get through work without incident. I did a good job, as I always do. Most of the time. Maybe I was a little more distant. That was to be expected. I was trying my best to pretend that everything was okay. Fake it until you make it. Smile and be love, until that is what surrounds you. You create your own reality. Is this what I had created?

I was walking home with a to-go box full of food for the next morning when a couple of young homeless kids asked me if I could spare any leftovers. I told them I could give them money. This was my breakfast. "No, just a little food would be nice." It was soup. Basically. Stew. Super wet. In a cardboard box. No utensils. I told them so, but gave it to them anyway. They were excited, and started to eat. The other one kept thanking me profusely, telling me about how the world could be a better place if everyone were like me. He stood there rambling at me while his friend ate. It was awkward. They looked like they had left school one day and never went back. They both had backpacks, wearing what most teenagers do (jeans and a t-shirt).

I saw them a few more times after that. Wondering what their story was. As I was walking home, I passed my new workplace, Louie's. It was good for that reason, really close to my apartment. I crossed the street so I could walk by the gate. Maybe I could talk to someone for a brief moment. Maybe she would be the closer. The gate was locked. I put my hand on the bars and looked in. Nothing.

Then I heard some kind of yell from the alley, where the staff entrance is. I ran toward it. A stupid thing to do really. If you hear screaming, you really shouldn't go towards it. You should go the other way. Fast. As I stood looking down the alley, I saw a man on the ground shielding his face. I didn't recognize him.

He was pulled under a car, out of sight, and a noticeable amount of liquid drained from where he had been taken. It was blood. His screams fell silent. I stared down the alley, taking slow, uneasy steps. I could feel heat on my chest where there was the cross I had been given as a child. I still wore it, though I believed in different things now. It was on fire. I wondered if my skin would be scarred from it, but that wasn't what I should be thinking about first and foremost. I saw a figure walk out from behind the car. It was Jenny.

She looked taller, but slouched over with her hands stretched out with claw-like fingers down to her knees. It was obscene. Something that I had only seen in movies. The bottom half of her face was covered in red liquid and her beautiful blue eyes were flaming red. Her hair looked like fiery red emeralds, darker than normal, but somehow glowing. She looked straight at me, where I was frozen. I couldn't move as she walked toward me. Was this going to be how I died? As she got closer her appearance started to return to normal.

Now she was half a foot away from me, her normal self, darling blue eyes, soft pale skin. Clotted blood spilled on her face. She looked like the cat who ate the canary. I couldn't say anything. She put her hand around my head and pulled me toward her, licking and sucking on my neck. My whole body was tingling. She looked me in the eyes and smiled, then kissed me gently. A peck at first, a gentle lick to test the waters. Then a full on kiss. She smelled as good as ever, tasting of iron and saliva. I licked the side of her face, tasting the blood of whomever it was under that car. She shuddered with pleasure and her eyes narrowed seductively.

I closed my eyes, feeling the pleasure tingling throughout my body. When I opened them, she was gone. She went... wherever it is creatures like her go. I hurriedly walked home to get a hold of myself. I brushed my teeth and washed my face, then poured water over the reddish-clear droplets that were in the sides of the sink from the blood that had washed off.

I stood there looking at myself in the mirror. The body who was myself. Identifying as such. As I walked to work the next day, I saw police tape around the alley at Louie's. It would be a few days before I saw her again, the next time I worked there. It had been real. I was sure I should feel horrified about what had happened, but I still had this longing, craving, love, this desire inside of me to be closer to her.

Conflict raged on in my mind, but I distanced myself from it, reasoning that I wasn't on the menu. I was lucky. She liked me. I had been chosen to survive this. We would be together after all.

Chapter 4
Don't Forget to Breathe

I still don't know what to do now. Life as usual, I guess. I feel like I have major anxiety built up inside of me and no way to let it out. It feels like someone inflated my head, and left some of the air. A soft pressure inside of my upper forehead. I have been working-out every day. They say endorphins will help you through times like these. I have been doing everything I'm supposed to. I wake up, exercise, meditate, feed and play with the cat, then go to work. It's the time in between when I'm not sure what to do with myself, that gets to me. I want to see her sooner than fate is allowing. I want to ask her what had happened. I want to tell her that I accept her, no matter how flawed she is. Even if that means she is a flesh-eating demon. I don't care. I know what it is like to be an outsider. I have an unfamiliar attachment to her, and I can tell somewhere in her the same feeling exists.

I sat on my couch after exercising, staring at my little orange cat. Gorgeous. What beautiful things there are in the world. His name is Ezekiel. I found him wandering the streets by my apartment and started feeding him. Now he is my faithful little companion. Always watching. I don't know how he could be comfortable, sitting on the arm of the couch, because his front paws were on the remote control for the television. This is what my life had come to. Staring, observing, watching. I felt no urges but the one to see her again. I knew I couldn't force it. I had to wait until she was ready. Or until our next day we worked together. Then the day came. I was there before her, anxious. When she came, I tried to play it cool, but could not resist hugging her and feeling her body against mine one more time. I could tell there was something on her mind.

"About last week," she said.

"It's okay," I told her, "I understand. I accept you for who you are."

"What? Really? I mean, my life is all kinds of messed up. I shouldn't be bringing someone else into it. I'm sorry that it happened the way it did."

"I'm not. I care about the real you, not just some show you have to put on. That's what we all do. We play our character all day at work, then with our families and friends. I don't want us to play roles with each other. I want us to be genuine."

"It's something I can't help. It's not like I want to do it or anything, it's just instinct. Sometimes it comes out and I can't control it."

"I feel the same way. I often had urges in the past that I did not give in to, though I wanted to. Sometimes I wonder what my life would be like if I had," I told her.

"How do you control your feelings?" she asked.

"It's not about controlling them. They will be there whether you want them to be or not. You just have to understand them and respect them. That means feeling bad sometimes, but never holding it in. If you accept and understand your needs, and where they come from, then you will be better able to move past them without hurting anyone."

"Can you teach me?" she asked.

"Yes, of course. I would be glad to."

"You're not worried that I might... hurt you?"

"No. You would have already, if you were going to."

"But this kind of thing, stopping it I mean, it intensifies. It builds and builds until it comes out, and I don't want it to be on you," she said.

"It's okay. My feelings for you are unconditional. If it means taking a few hits, that is fine with me. Come home with me after work tonight, we can go through a guided meditation."

"Okay," she said, reluctantly agreeing. I could tell she was a very logical person, with very strong feelings for what she believed. It was going to be hard to convince her that everything would be okay with me. I never doubted, but it's hard to get past that sort of logic dominated mind, the one that thinks running is going to solve your problems. Instead it just leaves a hole where something beautiful could have been planted.

After work she came to my apartment. I lit a stick of incense and offered it to the figures on my table. She told me about her past and the spiritual alignments that were forced upon her by her family. I told her I experienced similar, but my family had been accepting of my change in identification, whereas hers had shut her out. It's sad that something that is supposed to make us better people often makes us worse. I told her my stance, which is that every religion is right and wrong. That we should just take the parts of all of them that celebrate life and existence, and pay homage to those, instead of the negative, judgmental aspects that breed hate. She told me that she didn't believe in anything anymore. That is the logical mind. If it exists, where is it? It doesn't seem to play much of a part in our day to day life. It does for me. We have to go within ourselves to see beyond this illusion of reality. She had to know there was more, if not, how did she explain her craving for flesh?

I let her have the cushion, and I sat on the floor with my legs crossed. I talked to her about the breathing exercises and guided her through them. It seemed to be going well. We were both relaxing. "It's like a storm in my head," she said. "All these thoughts, coming and going all the time."

"The first thing is to realize them," I said. "Don't get involved. Let them come and go without interacting. Once you can see them, you can separate from them." We sat there in silence for ten more minutes. Then I felt her hand on mine. I opened my eyes. She leaned in and kissed me. I kissed her back. She pushed me over onto the ground and got on top of me. She was biting my neck again, our hands feeling all over each other, pulling us as close together as we could. This was one outlet. My mind was silent. We took off each other's shirts and the feeling of flesh on flesh was driving me mad. Her taste. Her scent. I loved every part of it. Only with the right person, can one enjoy these things so absolutely. She was the right one.

"We can't," she said. "We have to wait."

"I know. I am just enjoying this. It means more to me," I said. This time wanting more, but knowing better. I really wanted us to build something special.

"Let's just go to sleep," she said. So we were in bed half naked, her in my arms. I could feel her heartbeat. I could taste her existence in my mouth and in my core. My head was silent, enjoying every second of the moment. Then I feel asleep. I woke up and sighed when she wasn't there next to me. She must have left during the night. Part of my heart had left along with her. It hurt inside my chest.

I fed Ezekiel and took a shower then headed to the living room, which was a mess. What had happened? All of my wine was taken out of the cooler and wood pieces were strewn about. Had someone broken in just to trash the place? I hope none of the wine went bad. Why had it been taken out? I should start with an explanation. A few months ago I purchased a wine refrigerator that was bigger than a normal refrigerator. It could hold three hundred bottles and was often referred to by me as the behemoth, or coffin, in my living room. I opened it, to find Jenny sitting inside. I kneeled down and put my hand on her face, rubbing it gently with my thumb. Her skin was chilled. Her eyes opened.

"This is how I sleep," she said, "I need it to be colder, darker, and confined."

"It's okay," I said, "I am happy you are here. How do you feel?"

"Frustrated. Pent up. Like I need a release."

"Like you want to kill someone?"

"No. Yes. I don't know. I have conflicting feelings about what I want and I feel like none of them are the answer. What is wrong with me?"

"Nothing is wrong with you. You are perfect the way you are. I like you because of who you are." I kissed her to stop her from saying more. She was torturing herself with her constant thoughts of things she couldn't control. If anyone needed to learn to be in the moment, it was her.

That's how I ended up with a demon sleeping in my wine fridge. A beautiful, red-haired, soft-skinned, goddess of a demon. Why did I feel like I was only ever in someone's life when they needed repair? I was happy to be there with her, but I couldn't help but feel like I didn't matter that much. We had coffee together then she left for work. Ezekiel walked out of the bedroom, giving me a look.

"Looks like we have another guest staying with us now," I said to him. He only meowed in reply. I took it as his acceptance, but he probably just wanted food.

Chapter 5
Silence in the Studio

The next day, Jenny texted me that she still felt like we couldn't be together. I think she was glossing over whatever it was that really bothered her. I kept getting the same objection even though she knew it didn't matter to me. There were so many reasons we shouldn't be together, but she was sticking with the weakest ones. I couldn't expect people to spend as much time as I did to try to understand themselves. That would be a losing battle. I know she had a lot going on in her life. She was older than me. I don't know why, but when you get older your choices go based on what is logical instead of following your heart. Social conventions, like age, override natural instinct. I never felt like anything mattered except for the connection between people. That is what I had found, a person. Someone I could connect with. I didn't care about her baggage, no matter how heavy it was. I know I should care. I saw someone die in front of me, but that was only a small issue. Feelings like this don't grow on trees. Much bigger things were still to follow.

I took it hard. Even though it had only been a few days. We hadn't even been intimate, beside the passionate hours spent making out, and when I saw her vulnerable. How was it so easy to turn off? I imagine that the turmoil in her life was much bigger than what had shaken up my world. Her. Feelings for her. Whatever they were. I thought I had been conscious, enjoying every moment of it, but somewhere along the way I assumed there would be more, and started to have expectations. No fair.

I talked to Zach about it at work that night. He told me that it sucks when things die before they ever had a chance, but that I had to understand it was all for the best. At least he didn't say she wasn't good enough for me. I knew that part on my own.

On the plus side, we did get our paychecks that night. Not that I cared. It was just a cycle of making money to pay to live. Money was just money. Loneliness just aloneness. I had to understand that. To find a way to get back where I had been. I was perfectly happy by myself and then she came into my life. It was her choice too. She kissed me first, but it takes two to tango. I went with it, even when I thought she was in a relationship. Ugh. I tried so hard to keep her off of my mind. Hardly a month ago I didn't even know she existed, and I was happy spreading loving awareness around my environment. I had only myself to blame. I expected too much from someone who was not ready to give it. To anyone else, and probably even herself.

I'm truly afraid now. I really am. Not because of that. There is something wrong with me. My head. My feelings. We speak of them as if we have a box with little creatures in it that we can take out and show people. Hey, look at this, I just got this one, it's an angry loathing. Wow. Look at that. I am still trying to find a loving awareness. Oh, nice. I had one of those a little while ago, but I haven't been able to find it. I think it changed into something that didn't feel as good. No, it's probably somewhere at the bottom of the box. You'll find him one day.

Chapter 6
The Bank

I kept thinking about her. Bet you didn't expect that. Even when it did stop, it started again, and I knew I would have to see her in a few days. Was I torturing myself by staying at my part time job? I would have quit. It didn't matter to me, but I knew that wasn't the real reason she didn't want to be closer to me. Jobs grew on trees for people like me. I could get a job at any restaurant. That wasn't the point. I guess I don't know what I expected. Only what I was willing to give, and that hadn't been enough. Maybe I should have been more forceful.

I was on my way to the bank to deposit my check. It was a beautiful day, as always, out here in Santa Fe. The sun was shining brightly as I walked down the street past the post office, only a few more blocks to the bank. There were nice flowers along the way. They were a combination of desert wild-flowers and man-made organisms that were planted well outside of their natural habitat. I was those flowers. Out of my environment. In society. Just like the plants I had on my porch. I have a Bodhi tree that is doing quite well, and just recently acquired a bleeding heart vine, which is the lucky flower of my Chinese zodiac. I don't know how much of that I believe, but it is enough that when combined with selective attention, confirmation bias, and coincidence, it seemed pretty accurate.

I was not happy that green was supposed to be unlucky for me. My eyes are green and I have always sided with the color. Red was their choice for me. Red of all the colors. The color of blood. Anger. Blah. It is supposed to be a lucky color in China. A color of power. Someone once told me that you are supposed to wear black and red into a job interview. That seemed too bold to me. People aren't the way they used to be. Hiring managers, I mean. Well, maybe it's just in my field. No manager is looking for an underling that is stronger than them, just someone who is really pleasant to be around and helpful. Team players instead of overachievers. Our jobs are so replaceable, I don't blame them. They think it matters. It's important to them to feel like they have control.

Ah, there I was at the bank, walking in through the sliding doors. There were a lot of people in line today. That means five. I think that is busy for them, even though they have almost ten registers. Three were open. Tellers waved their hands, beckoning the next person to step up. It was pretty fast here. Then my whole world collapsed. This time it was in my mind, a little later for real. It was almost my turn when Jenny walked in through the doors. She didn't look happy. My chest started burning like it had that night. It was the cross I was wearing. I'll always remember that feeling. That warning. I started to ask her how she was, but it was too late to ask. Her fingers were getting longer with claw-like protrusions. Her hair was catching fire again, almost blinding to look at the brilliant orange-red that complimented her now blood red eyes that could burn a hole through your heart. I heard a few gasps around me. My heart was beating so fast, it felt like it had stopped. She swung her arm at me and struck my shoulder hard. I was physically thrown across the room and into a wall. I hit my head. My glasses flew off of my face. I blacked out for I don't know how long.

When I looked up, things were blurry, but I could tell that people were screaming and being ripped apart. I saw dark red streams of liquid that must have been blood. I could hear the alarm going off. It wasn't the silent type. A red figure flew across the room at a woman who was trying to leave. Screaming. Crunching. Silence. I saw the two red dots of her eyes staring at me, though I couldn't see her clearly without my glasses. There was a yell from across the room as some brave soul had picked up one of the divider poles and was swinging it like he was fighting off a lion. She pounced on him. He was yelling, "help, help," but everyone knew there was nothing they could do. I pulled myself on my stomach through the doors and outside. The sun burned away at my face. My body hurt like fuck. I managed to stumble to my feet and ran at a slow jog, holding my shoulder the whole time, as I felt blood flowing down the side of my face. I was completely disoriented. I had to go down side streets, too many people would see me on the main road. I went the back way and cut through the park. I couldn't see well enough without my glasses to know if anyone was watching. Looking over my shoulder every so often, to see if the glowing eyes were coming. No one seemed to be following me. I didn't know if I should be more afraid of her or the police. How could I explain this. I really couldn't see that well. It didn't matter.

I got through the gate into my apartment complex and went to my car where there was an extra pair of glasses. I got into the passenger seat and opened the center console. I couldn't move my right arm without it hurting so I was digging through the console with my left hand, pulling everything out onto the driver seat. Then I found the spare glasses I had in there. I put them on and could see clearly. I pulled down the visor and looked in the mirror. The whole right side of my face was covered in blood. It looked bad. The part of me that was cut bled profusely. It was one of those spots that liked to bleed. Right by the eyebrow. I felt like I was hit by a car. Hunched over, holding up my right arm as I walked, I managed to get into my apartment. I was just entering the hallway when I saw a figure passing by the picture-window. I held myself against the wall, where I wouldn't be seen. My heart was racing, probably making my head bleed more. It hurt so much. I wondered if she could hear the way I was breathing. Peeking slightly around the corner, I saw the tall lanky figure outside of the window. As she put her cupped hands against the window and looked in, I hid myself once more in the hallway. Just breathe. It will go away. What was happening? How did I invite this into my life? There were red spots of blood on the window where she had looked in. Her eyes were blue again. She was beautiful either way, but I couldn't let her in. Not this time. I could hear sirens in the distance. I closed my eyes and fell to the ground, blacking out again.

Chapter 7

Pain

I woke up in my bed the next day. I must have crawled there during the night. When I got up, which was somewhat of a painful struggle, having to avoid using the right half of my body, I hobbled to the bathroom, and turned on the light. My face was still bloodied. It looked like I had lost a fight. A big fight. I had lost something. It would be okay. I would take a shower and everything would be alright. It would heal on its own. I took a shower. It hurt. Pain in places I didn't know I had bruises. There was a big circle of skin missing on my hand. Scrapes on my elbow, knee, and hip. My shoulder hurt the most. The cut on my face burned with the water contact, but the bleeding had stopped. I was clean. I put first aid cream on the cuts and covered them. I sat on my couch trying to watch television but not getting into it. I went back to bed. Woke up a few hours later, my body still in pain. I looked at the wound on my face. Okay. Maybe I do need stitches.

I looked up the nearest urgent care center that took my health insurance and braced myself for the feat that was before me. Luckily it was only two miles, but I had to drive with one hand, taking it slow for sure. I made it there and filled out the paperwork. Two different people asked me what happened. I told the same story. Yesterday, as I was walking home from work, I was crossing the street and a car ran the red light, hitting me, then driving away. I didn't feel that bad at the time, though I was probably in a bad mindset, which is why I walked home instead of going to the hospital. I couldn't give them any details about the car. It had been completely unexpected, catching me off guard. I was glad to be alive. Lucky to be alive. They asked me all kinds of questions to see if I had a concussion, but it seemed that I didn't, even though my brain was fried. It was hard for me to think.

I couldn't concentrate enough to read anything or even watch television earlier that day. They did x-rays of my arm and glued the laceration on my head. They asked me if I wanted to fill out a police report, but I told them there was no point because there was nothing to go on beside that it had happened. They said I would be okay. I told them how much pain I was in but they just told me to take any over the counter pain killer for it. They gave me a prescription for antibiotics so I wouldn't get an infection from the cuts. I was in the clear. At least from the doctors and possibly authorities. Not from her. She would be back.

I sat and waited for the prescription at the drug store that was in the same plaza. Then drove back home again with one hand, narrowly avoiding a few cars on the way. I sat back down on the couch. Tried to watch a movie again. Still wasn't going through. I had to call off of work that day and the next. I could barely lift a glass of water at this point, though every day it was feeling a little better. The opposite came with appearance. Every day it looked a little worse for the next five days. More black and blues started showing up, more yellow spots all over my right side. I kept icing it and bandaging the wounds. The day after that, I did go to work. They were all shocked, having never seen anything like this from me. I was a pretty healthy person. I managed to get through it, doing as little with my right arm as possible. I didn't mind people asking me what had happened until three days later when I kept seeing more people and they just kept asking. The next day I had a double at Louie's. Where I was sure to see her. Jenny. Maybe I should just not show up. I could call off. No. I have to face it eventually. I have to face her, eventually. They let me go home first in between shifts. Everyone there gave me hugs and showed sympathy. Some of the older patrons cowered in fear at me when I smiled to them. I had never experienced that before. I always saw myself as love. Now I was instilling fear. Intimidating to look at. People probably assumed the worst. That I was an angry person, who liked to fight people. Not that the truth was much better. I saw Jenny.

She asked me what happened, as if she didn't know. I told her my story of being hit by a car and got her sympathy as well. Not as much as I wanted. I wanted her to pick me up and carry me home. I wanted to spend the day in her arms, feeling better or dying. A beautiful scene in my living room until it got too late and she had to sleep in my wine fridge. But that didn't happen. We moved on to the next subject, when I asked her about her life. She was eager to talk about herself. I made it through the night. At work. Taking medicine as needed. They gave me the last tables. I stayed and closed with her and got two hugs, this time, before having to walk home. I deserved it. She told me she was sorry that this happened to me. I was too. I guess that was the closest I would get to an apology.

The next day I worked again. I felt worse this day. My very existence was aching. New pains had started in my side and ribs. My head was not in the good place it had been the day before. Everyone was irritable. They gave me the most tables. I did at least double the guests everyone else did and made the most money. Good. I would need it to pay medical bills. I didn't wait for her that night. Everyone was being rude to everyone else. It felt like she didn't even want to look at me. Fine. I texted her later asking if she was okay, but got no response.

Summary Report
Third of August
National Bank on Guadalupe St.
Twelve confirmed dead
Officer on duty: Lieutenant John Stevens

I arrived at the scene with my partner at approximately 4 P.M. to find no survivors. It was gruesome. Photos of the crime scene confirm the death of seven National Bank employees, and five civilians. Cash boxes and vault appear untouched. No money was taken from the bank. Security cameras show a Caucasian male, approximately six feet tall, mid to late twenties was the first one attacked by some unearthly force. After that, the cameras inside the bank were fried by something unknown. May have been a power surge, but that doesn't explain it in my opinion. We have video of the Caucasian male being thrown across the room and then... nothing. A street camera by the entrance shows this man crawling out of the building. If he is still alive, he is our best lead. We have no evidence of whether or not one of the bodies inside was his, but do not believe so, as of now. They were too badly disfigured to identify by appearance. I don't know what could have done this. It had to be something from another world. It certainly couldn't have been human.

Lieutenant Stevens

Re: Summary Report, National Bank

Officer Stevens, this report is unacceptable. You know we can't have things like 'unearthly forces' as the cause of a massive homicide like this. Please reconsider your choice in words. I agree that there aren't many things that could tear a person apart like I saw in the crime scene photos. Please re-submit your report with something feasible, like a wolf or bear attack. I can't send things like this to the main office and expect them to take us seriously. I'm sure I don't have to tell you to make it a priority to find the survivor and see if he can offer a rational explanation.

-Captain Phelps

Re: Re: Summary Report, National Bank

Understood sir. I will resubmit it tomorrow morning.

-Lieutenant Stevens

Chapter 8

It Just Hurt so Much

Everything still hurt, but it was getting better. I was taking care of it as best as I could. It was my day off. I could finally sit here and do nothing. Recovering more. I had been doing all that I could to make it better. I meditated constantly and did reiki on my whole body. I am a level two practitioner. I prayed. Asked for help in healing my body and mind. It was hard. Not just feeling like this, but the mental state that came with it. It was scary to leave my house. To walk by the places I had been before, hoping I would be okay. It made me sick to my stomach to go near the bank. My car still smelled like blood. I had spent two days after the incident cleaning blood off of the carpet, walls, and front walkway. I was doing everything I could to heal. I played healing and protection mantras on YouTube, listening to them while I was home.

I meditated, doing special meditations to ward off negative energy and bad spirits. I used special vibhuti, ceremonial powder, on my body to blind spirits from me. I prayed on positive energy and healing powers. I thanked God I was alive. It was the sixth day. I could move my arm all the way now, though it did hurt. I wouldn't be able to lift anything for a while. I was sitting on my couch resting when she came to my door again. There was no hiding this time, and I was craving her. Her scent came to my nose when I thought about her. I had to understand what was going on. She brought a dozen red roses for me. Beautiful blood red. Wet blood. Not the dried blood I had just cleaned off the window, that had become almost brown. It was a feel better gift. Sitting next to her on the couch, I could feel her energy. It was not displeasing. My cross was not burning this time. There was no warning necessary. She wasn't here to kill me, though I welcomed death over suffering.

"I hate to see you like this," she said to me. "You know I can make it all go away if you let me."

"What do you mean?" I asked her.

"Your wounds. You shouldn't let them hurt like that. I can take care of them if you let me heal you. You just have to ask."

"Alright, go ahead. Heal me."

"I can't, it's the cross. You have to take off your cross for me to help you." That was a bad sign. Alarm bells should have been ringing in my head, but I had already surrendered myself to her completely. What manner of energy was this? What if it was all that was protecting me from her? I could hear Zach's voice in my head telling me what I was doing was wrong. Ezekiel watched us from across the room looking disapprovingly at us. I think he wanted the attention that I was giving Jenny. It wasn't the pain that was the biggest motivator, but the need to be closer to her. I wanted her to eat my heart, but not literally. I wanted our hearts to be connected. Though half the time she seemed to not even care if I existed. Reaching for my cross, I remembered my dad's words when he had given it to me. "You have to wear this at all times. It is for protection. Let it guide you through life." I lifted the chain over my head and placed the cross on the coffee table.

"That wasn't so hard, was it?" Jenny asked me. She had a big smile on her face, like she was capable of anything. She jumped on me, pushing me over onto my back and ripped through my shirt. She took her top off and I could feel her hot body pressing against mine as she bit down on the side of my neck like she had the last time we were making out. I knew it would be different this time. It hurt, but felt good. Her tongue was long, as it felt its way over my shoulder where the worst pain was. She put her hand over it and gripped it tightly, which was not the most pleasant feeling I had ever had. It felt like fire shooting through my whole body. The bruises burned the worst. She pulled the bandage from my face and licked it before kissing me deeply. I wrapped my arms around her, ignoring the pain in my arm, trying my best to get her closer to me even though our bodies were touching. I felt her body being pulled against me tightly, ecstatically. Electricity running through me. My vision went white and everything was gone. I woke up on the couch. Alone again. Had that really happened? My ripped shirt was still on the ground by the coffee table. The cat was sleeping next to me. The pain was gone. Everything had healed. She was right. I couldn't help but feel like she was part of me now. I put the cross back on and meditated by my altar, using the sacred ash once again to make me invisible to spirits.

Chapter 9

Connectivity

I could feel her in my bloodstream. We would always have this connection. When I got close to her at work I could feel it burning in me. My whole body would get hot. It felt like my skin was going to ignite, but it never did. The hair on my arms would stand up in excitement when we made eye contact. I wondered how hot my skin would be to the touch, but it felt normal to me. That wouldn't be the only thing that had changed about me. Apparently when you share energy with a demon you gain some of its power.

That or it unlocks secret power you already have, but never knew about. I would theorize that it burns through some of the walls of reality that keep humans separated from ethereal beings. I thought the sex was going to be great when it happened, but this was already one step beyond such base instinct. That was all Earthly reality. This was Godly. Did this mean that all of the fairytales I had heard in my life were true? Dante's Inferno. Faust. The Bible. Would I have to be open to believe all of them in a literal sense? It would be hard to deny now, but one does not necessarily follow the other. Maybe it is just a genetic mutation that makes some people different from others. That means there are some with horns that look stupid and don't have any powers. Nature is like that. Not always improving us for social settings.

Everyone at the restaurant was telling me how well it had healed and that I was lucky. I felt that way too. She smiled at me across the bar when I came to get drinks for my tables. I smiled back, having less to say than usual. I was still getting used to the feelings I was having. They were beyond anything I had felt for anyone else in my life. It just takes one ethereal being to shatter your whole world-view, and that of the dating scene. Nothing would ever be the same. Is this what Stockholm Syndrome feels like?

As I was standing by the service bar waiting for the drinks to be poured into the rest of the glasses in front of me, her elbow brushed against one of the champagne flutes. It started falling over toward me, in my periphery. I grabbed out at it instinctively and managed to catch it. That's not the strange part. The strange part is that the sparkling wine that had been spilling had stayed in the air and casually threw itself back into the glass when I made eye contact with it.

"Nice catch. Did you do that or did I?" Jenny asked.

"It was you," I said. Believing that her presence inside of me was responsible for this. Not catching the glass, but controlling the liquid.

"This is such a bad idea," she had said to me that night we were standing out in the rain. She kept repeating it over and over like I didn't understand what she said the first time. I think she was trying to convince herself. But this was good. It's not like I was hurting anyone and it wasn't my place to judge the things that she did. I loved her. Now I even had super powers on top of that. Sure, some people would have to die, but they would have died either way. Whether I was involved or not. It wasn't my choice. It was God's choice. The universe. Karma. Whatever you want to call it. It was their time. That's all. You can't blame a bear for killing, why blame a demon?

I was excited for this newfound tele-kinesis. Though I couldn't control it at this point. Things like the levitating champagne happened a few more times that night, and would now be a regular part of my life. The only caveat, is that it didn't work on people. When I felt it coming, I tried to direct it toward someone writing the tip, but it didn't work. For some reason it wouldn't work on living things. There must have been something about their energy field that prohibited my interference. Maybe it was some universal idea of freewill. For normal objects, I could feel and connect with them, then manipulate what was happening.

The first few days of having this power, I tried to use it as often as I could in order to gain control over it. It worked. I figured out how to activate it and could already manipulate it. I sat on my couch and brought my mug of coffee to my hands without ever lifting a finger. I levitated the cats toys above Ezekiel and down the hall so that he could chase them and get exercise. I mentally used the television remote to turn on my favorite show. It was a neat parlor trick. The novelty wore off pretty fast, but I could see that it would be useful once in a while. I could probably use this at a casino... but that would be too suspicious. I am a good person. I was never trying to take advantage of anyone. I worked hard and made the money that I was owed. It would have been nice to win the lottery, but I could never take money from someone directly without working for it. One thing was for sure, it wasn't something that I would be able to show to anyone except for those closest to me. I don't know how I would be able to explain it to future loved ones and family. I was beginning to think that I had to move on from Jenny. She wasn't giving me much of a choice, though the moments we shared were above anything I had experienced before.

The next day at my main job, Chez Fe, I told Zach about it. The whole thing. When I got there he looked concerned, which was an expression most people hadn't been wearing since my face healed.

"What happened to your face?" he asked. Again, something most people had said when I had bruises. Had they come back? I would have to look in the mirror. Somehow I felt like they were still gone.

"What do you mean?" I asked.

"Don't play dumb, the last time you were here you had a black eye and a big gash in your forehead. Not to mention your arm. You could barely lift a glass of water."

"It got better."

"Yeah, I see that. How?"

"You remember that girl I talked to you about?"

"Yes. What does she have to do with it?"

"She healed me."

"She healed you?"

"Yes."

"And how exactly did she do that?"

"She licked the wounds and they healed themselves."

"Really? Just like that? You didn't have to do anything in return?"

"No, I mean she likes me. I like her. I just took off my cross and she healed it for me."

"Aha! I knew there was more to it. That's bad. I know you feel better and are healed, but anything that requires you to take off your cross is probably not a good thing, bud. I love you and I want to see you okay, but that is something you have to watch out for. You have to promise me you won't take it off again."

"What? I mean, I was reluctant too, but it all worked out okay. What's the big deal?"

"Taking off a relic such as this opens you up to the influence of all sorts of forces in the world. Good and bad. You wear this talisman to ward off anything that might not be so nice."

"I guess that's why I wear it, yeah, my parents gave it to me when I was little. They said it would protect me."

"It will. You just can't take it off. Promise me you won't."

"Okay, I won't take it off."

"Is that all that happened?"

"Yes. Well, no. Look at this," I said, pulling out a pen. I held it up in the palm of my hand, then made it levitate.

"Jesus, man. You can't do things like that. People are going to think you're crazy," Zach said. "I told you there would be consequences. If anyone finds out about this, our whole world could come crashing down."

I appreciated his sentiment. That we were figuratively brothers. I was glad to have someone in my life who cared about me. Who would believe me. He was always someone I could depend on. He had a family of his own and always did what he thought was best for them. He was right. I shouldn't have taken it off. I should have gone through the pain... but I don't regret it. At all. I love her. I am healed. I have superpowers. What's to be upset about? I would just try to minimize the amount of things I moved with my mind in public. It wouldn't be that hard to seem normal. I had been doing it my whole life.

The rest of the night went by smoothly. There weren't that many people in town anymore, so two servers was more than enough. When everything was cleaned and the paperwork done, Zach offered me a ride home, which I politely declined. I was all the way to the end of the street when two guys made their presence known to me. They had been waiting under the stairwell that lead to the Cantina, a restaurant I didn't often visit. Normally I would have kept walking, but something was burning inside of me, causing me to make all the wrong decisions.

"Where do you think you're going?" one of them asked, pulling out a knife. The other had his hands in his pockets, something that was probably a gun was bulging in the front. The one with the knife walked over to me and asked for my wallet, not very politely even.

"What are you smiling at?" he asked me, "You think something's funny about this?" I couldn't help but smile. They picked the wrong person, on the wrong day. I could feel Jenny's power flowing throughout my body. I felt like I could take on anything at this point.

"Just cut him and get this over with," said the other thug, who was still under the stairwell.

The man in front of me wasn't very big. He was a few inches shorter than me even. He had short hair, shifty panicked eyes. People who do this kind of thing are always projecting their own fear out into the world. I wasn't afraid of him. He pushed the knife forward toward me, but I quickly reached out and grabbed it by the blade. I wrapped my hand around it tightly, feeling it cutting into me. He stared into my eyes trying to pull the knife away and I stared back, holding onto it. The fire was burning inside of me. Flames. I was on the verge of blacking out from the intensity of it. Would she come and save me? I wanted her to take me away from here, away from everyone. Just us, alone together.

"Let go!" he yelled at me, looking more and more bothered. He punched me across the face, with the hand not holding the knife. My new glasses flew to the ground. I turned my head back to look at him again.

I could see everything clearly. I was seeing through something different than my own eyes at this point. A darkness inside of me that wouldn't let me be the victim anymore. He could see this had been a mistake. The thug under the stairwell took a step forward and brought his hand out of his pocket, pointing a gun at me. He was shaking it out in front of him as if he could direct traffic with it. I just smiled back at him while the other guy tried to get his knife back. I wanted that gun. I imagined myself holding it. I am holding the gun. I wanted to use my new powers to steal it from him. The darkness was growing. My teeth felt funny. Maybe I had been grinding them. It was like they were different somehow, sharper, ready to be of use to me. I could feel my fingernails protruding, becoming claws, my teeth fangs. Jenny was coming out in me.

Before we could continue, a jeep started up the alley toward us, honking it's horn. Zach was driving this way. He had been hanging out in his car and was now headed home.

The thug in front of me let go of the knife and started to run. His friend pulled the trigger. I saw it in slow motion, the flash of the gunpowder exploding, sending out it's projectile of hot metallic death. My body jerked back and I fell to the ground as the jeep pulled up to me. The man with the gun ran for it. Zach got out and took a few steps yelling, but knew he couldn't go after the man with the gun. He ran over to me to see if I was okay. My mouth ached. My fingers ached. My hand hurt. There was a cut across it from the knife. Sitting up, I asked him for my glasses. I couldn't see very well without them. Putting them on, I let Zach take my arm and help me to my feet.

"Are you alright?" he asked. "You sure are lucky I was driving by."

That was one way to look at it. I was lucky. They were lucky.

"I guess he missed," I said. "He probably wasn't trying to hit me, but just to scare us." I held out my hand, showing him the wound from the knife. "My hand wasn't so lucky." I looked at him and started laughing. He shook his head.

"We have to get that wrapped up," he said. "Get in the car."

I walked toward the passenger seat and waited while he opened the door from the inside. The locks were manual, and I couldn't open it from the outside. It was the perfect distraction, while he was doing that, I looked in my other hand at the bullet I had caught, and let it fall to the ground before getting in the jeep. When I got in the car, I felt myself sitting on something hard. It was in my belt in the back. I felt it, without pulling it out. It was the gun.

Chapter 10
Chains that Bind Them

The wound was starting to heal. The one on my hand from holding onto the knife. Not as fast as the last one. I hadn't seen Jenny since this happened. I wondered if she would be proud. I doubted it. Even if I had ripped their throats out, the way she had that night in the alley, I somehow felt like she would judge me for it. Do as I say, not what I do kind of thing. It was her energy that was coming out in me. As much as I wanted her to come and heal it for me, I remembered what Zach said, and agreed with him. I shouldn't have to compromise myself to open up to someone. It was starting to feel weaker. The feeling of her energy that had been burning in me. I couldn't make things float anymore. I felt weaker. The power that I had been enjoying made me feel like a deity. Now I was regular old me again. Maybe there was something I could do to hold on to what was left of it.

I had worked with energy previously in my life. Through meditation, and practicing reiki. It gave me an understanding of what it felt like when energy moved through your body. With focus I could feel it, and understand it. That led to being able to control it. It had always been my energy up until I met Jenny. Sharing with her was like opening the floodgates after years of rain. So much more than I was used to. I thought the best course of action would be to find another relic from an authentic source, so I headed downtown to the Tibetan antique store. There were at least ten such stores around town and only a few of them were authentic, carrying real

46

relics from the ancient lands. I had also read that these things could be dangerous, but at this point in my life, it didn't seem like a piece of metal or rock would be something to worry about. It was the flesh that concerned me.

As I opened the door and took a step into the import store, I noticed a big white dog lying on the floor to the left of the path. It was a small cube-shaped store with an island in the middle. There was a clerk behind a register in the back left corner. Genuine artifacts lying all around, looking like things you would find in rich people's homes instead of the temples they had come from.

The dog looked up at me and wagged his tail a bit, but was otherwise unmoved from his resting place. I said hi to the dog, which prompted the clerk to go on his usual speech.

"He is the owner. Since he is here, you can have fifteen percent off, today only," said the clerk. The same speech he had given every time I had come in, for the past five years. It was better when he was there. Sometimes there was an older woman who didn't offer the same discount. I never found out his name. I assumed he owned the store along with his wife, but only one of them was ever there at a time. I smiled and thanked him, then went looking through things in the store. There was a large pile of imported incense, straight from Tibet. The real deal. It was much too large for the little incense burners we have here. There were small statues of Buddhas and other Tibetan entities, that I was not as familiar with. I'm sure one must have been Tara. I knew more about the Hindu deities such as Shiva, Krishna, and Rama.

There was a little bowl of wrist bracelets (mala) that they had just brought back. The owners had recently returned from their annual trip to Tibet to retrieve more goods that they could sell to tourists.

"These are nice," I said, looking through the pile in the bowl. "But do you have anything stronger?"

"Stronger? What do you mean?" the clerk asked. He wasn't ready to have this conversation with me, just yet.

"Yes. Something real, authentic, and preferably red. I am looking for something to cycle power with."

"Ah. I see. That is very dangerous. Are you sure you know what you are doing?" I flew over to the register and grabbed him by his wrist. I could see in his eyes that he could feel it.

"Need I say more?" I asked him, letting go. He pulled away and rubbed his wrist with his other hand. I could see him thinking it over, and hoped I hadn't hurt him.

"Okay," he said. "I have something for you." He turned around to a small altar that had incense burning and rummaged through the relics that were stacked on it. Turning back to me, he showed me a mala for my wrist. "This is fire agate," he said, slowly rotating the bracelet in his hands so I could see all the details. It was a dark orange-brown color that looked a bit like salmon roe. "This is known as the spiritual flame of absolute perfection. It contains deep hidden secrets and ignites when you wear it. Be careful with this, it can stir up your emotions. You must be level headed when you use it. I chose this for you because it is known to increase energy. This particular one comes at a high price because of the circumstances in which it was obtained. Let's just say, the last person to wear it was not so fortunate."

"I don't mind paying what you ask," I told him.

"The money is not important," he said. Though I did end up paying more than I expected. "You must take these along with it, I insist." He handed me a second wrist mala, this one plain brown, sandalwood, and a bundle of sage. "The sage will help keep high vibrational rates around you, warding off anything that could be harmful to you. The wooden mala is a traditional Buddhist mala. It will help keep you grounded so that you will not fly too far if the energy grows beyond your means."

"Thank you," I said, handing him my credit card. He insisted on wrapping everything nicely and putting it into a bag, though I was ready to wear this newly acquired relic.

When I got home, I opened the bag and unwrapped the mala. I sat down at my meditation table and lit a stick of incense. I took a few deep breaths to relax, before putting on the mala. The ordinary wooden one acted as such. It was ascetically pleasing, but nothing happened. As one would expect. The fire agate acted quite differently. When I put it on, the orange-brown color changed to a deep red. It came to life, looking completely different than it had before. It fit snugly to my wrist, as if it had changed size to connect with me. I could feel energy traveling up my arm, into my body. I put my hands together to see what it would feel like. A switch was activated. I could feel it flowing through me. The power was there. This is exactly what I had wanted. I held my hands out toward the altar and a few of the statues started vibrating. I could feel myself being lifted as energy traveled through my body. Everything felt lighter. I felt stronger. She wouldn't slip away from me that easily.

Chapter 11
Working Myself Up

Finally the day came. I don't know why I didn't just quit. I think it was because of the money. It was time to go back to Louie's and I knew she would be working that night too. I kept seeing things out of the corner of my eye again. Not sure what it is. Maybe I should have gotten the anti-reflective coating on my new glasses. I wish it were that simple of an explanation.

My day had been going well up to this point. Not that it got that much worse just yet. I took a shower, had lunch, sat on the couch watching Ezekiel throw his fake chirpy bird all around the living room. Not the most productive, but it was relaxing sitting there listening to music. For some reason I really liked watching Ezekiel play with the toy bird. A hunter at heart. Ready for the real thing. My friend always told me he would bring one to my house one day. I would not be okay with that. Even after what I witnessed with Jenny. I have always felt like animals are more innocent than we are. Like they don't deserve to die. Even if it is "natural."

I got there before her. Servers always arrive before the bartenders. Why couldn't I get her out of my head? It was an obsession at this point for someone who didn't deserve my attention. Everyone else was always good to me. The dinner shift was uneventful. She did eventually come, gave me a hug, and we promptly worked together, doing our best to ignore each other throughout the night, except when I tried to be diplomatic and ask her about herself. I should have been meditating more often, the emotions I was feeling were extreme. She told me her ex-boyfriend was coming to town that night. I thought she meant later, but as it turns out, he would be drinking for free at the bar before the night was over.

The host said it best, "I don't remember her dating anyone so unattractive." His words, not mine. None of the full-on managers were there at night, which meant more fun for us. Usually that was a glass of wine after the shift. If they had anything tolerable. I was known for being a wine snob. Having good taste makes other people think you are pompous. I stand by it because the last time I drank one of their wines it gave me the worst hangover I have had in years. I feel like it is less pure, like drinking liquor that has been distilled multiple times. The aging process makes it more manageable. Things break down. I don't know the technical explanation for it. Good wine just doesn't have the same taste of alcohol that bad wine does. Good wine doesn't taste like alcohol, it tastes like pleasure, if pleasure was a flavor.

I knew I shouldn't expect much from her that night. She would probably take him home with her. I assumed that is the type of person she was. That and overhearing her saying things like she really needed to get laid and was craving sexuality. A slap in the face to me. I know she didn't mean for me to overhear. Don't ever let anyone tell you that older people are more mature. Especially than you. I'm sure a lot of people who have been married can tell you how strange it is to have so much love, and yet so much hate, for the same person.

When I was done I left. I didn't stay and have a drink. I didn't want to be around them, but I really wanted a drink, so I went to the nearest bar. Probably looking for the same thing that she was. Escape. Freedom. Love.

Sometimes I feel like I need to get away from myself. Like I don't really know who I am anyway.

After a few drinks and about forty minutes, I was sufficiently buzzed. It doesn't take much after work, especially with the high elevation and lack of food for the last six hours. They feed us at the beginning of the shifts there. All of the other bars were closing, so it was time for the last call bar. The one you only go to after drinking enough at other places to be able to stand going in there. It was by the railroad, a ten minute walk or so. I never drink and drive. I walk. That is one of the reasons I chose to live here. The crap bar! Warehouse club type place. As much as you can have that in Santa Fe. They checked my ID at the door, as always, and let me in. I feel like if his mother came, he would ID her. It was weird how any bar would let me in no matter how many drinks I had before I came, as long as I had my ID. They should probably have better sobriety tests in places where alcohol offenses are so serious. So I sat there with a beer watching the band play, looking around. Then she came in. Not just her. Her and her stupid unattractive ex-boyfriend. They sat at the bar talking to each other. Oh, God, what did I do to deserve this? Misery me. Now I have to watch her try to get her ex into bed. This bar is for people with no self-respect. None whatsoever. How do I end up in situations like this? I had to leave, but I couldn't let her win. Not like this. I had to show her that I didn't care.

I paid my tab, then on the way out walked up to both of them at the bar. Even in this state of intoxication, my body was in a panicked state. My heart racing. Mind going silent. I gave her a half hug that friends give and shook the guy's hand. Said hello, hoped they were enjoying their night. Then left. That was all it had to be. I knew she would feel like an asshole just knowing that I knew. Good. She should feel that way. She is the one making the poor decisions in life, not me. I smiled widely as I walked away, imagining them staring at my back. It probably only took a few more drinks before it never even happened in their minds, but I was victorious. The walk home felt a lot shorter than normal because of how good I was feeling.

I was just outside of my apartment. Excited to see my little orange cat come running when I opened the door. It had been years, but he would always do it. It was nice being somebody's whole world. Even if it was just Ezekiel. I struggle for a moment to get the key into the lock. The light was never on outside of my apartment, so it was sometimes difficult to maneuver, regardless of the drinking. I walked into the dark apartment and took my shoes off, after locking the door. Realize that I do this in complete darkness. There is no indoor light switch until I am all the way across the room. The only light comes from the picture-window, which now has some illumination from lights around the complex. They aren't that bright, and your eyes have to adjust when coming into complete darkness. Also, the lights had been off for a month or so at the time because they were working on the electricity. I couldn't see the cat run out from the hallway. I made it to the light switch, but adjusted the dimmer to low before turning them on. How could I have missed it? It all came to me at once. Her scent. Her image. She was sitting there on the couch. For how long? Had she left him and driven back here? Acting natural, I took off my shoulder bag and winter coat.

"I didn't expect to see you here," I said to her.

"That wasn't very nice of you, at the bar," Jenny replied.

It was uncomfortable how attractive I found her, sitting on my couch, looking the way she did. It wasn't just plain her. She was half transformed. Slight claws, a very gentle glow, and eyes that were still in transition.

"I was going to say the same to you," I replied.

"Don't you remember the last time we were on this couch together? How we kissed and fondled one another?"

"You are the one who wanted to stop seeing me, as I recall."

"There are things you don't understand."

"I think I understand all that I need to."

"You don't. I know you need me here with you. I know you want it. Crave it. I know it eats away at you the way we interact."

"Yes. It does," I said, trying not to overreact. Was she trying to make me upset?

"You have to let me be my own person. I have my own life."

"I could be a part of it if you wanted me to. Wanted it enough to make space for me."

"It's not that easy."

"But you are here now. Am I supposed to accept this?"

"You don't have to, but I hope you will. I can't be here all the time. You have to give me space. I will come when I can and when I must."

"You feel forced to be around me? Then why bother?"

"It's not like that. I am a part of you. We have this connection with each other that other people will never have."

"I know. I knew that the moment I kissed you. Why is this supposed to be news to me?" I sat down next to her on the couch. On her right side. The same way we had been sitting the last time she had come over. There was no music this time. Just the loud mechanics of the wine-fridge keeping itself cold. It came on a lot more often without wine in it. I guess I only kept it plugged in for her at this point. We didn't have any more to say to each other. She stared at me with her blackening eyes, hollow and empty, but so deep that I could get lost in them. Our faces got closer together, close enough to kiss, then she turned away.

"We just can't right now," she said.

Jenny got up from the couch. I stayed there, falling back into it, deeper and deeper. It was one of those Alice in Wonderland couches that could swallow you into another world if you let it. Jenny took a step forward and opened the door to the wine fridge. She took a step in and closed it behind her. I sat there on the couch, staring up at the ceiling, my head spinning. Ezekiel sat down next to me on my right side. He just sat there looking into nothingness. I followed in suit. My mind didn't know what to make of this.

Chapter 12
Zach
(From his perspective)

I heard the buzz of the phone trying to connect, then a familiar voice.

"Hello," said the voice.

"Hi. My name is Zach. I'm part of the Association," I replied.

"Are you in immediate danger?"

"No, I just need to talk to the elders."

"Anything not immediate must be sent electronically using the protocol. This line is not secured."

"I know, I just," there was a click. He had hung up. I would have to do it electronically.

To: The Association
Subject: Investigation into Unregistered Being

To Whom it May Concern:

My name is Zach. Registration number 3693. I have reason to believe there is an unregistered being violating the articles of our agreement with the commons.

An associate of mine has recently described meeting this being, of unknown origin, at his alternate place of employment, Louie's Bar & Grille. He has told me stories that must be relayed in person, not in writing. The being is believed to have attacked between one and ten people in the past few weeks, according to the stories. My friend is a credible source. He is registered, though he does not know it. His stories check out with local news reports, as well as strange circumstances involving transference of power.

I am taking immediate action into the investigation of the unregistered, who goes by the name "Jenny."

I recommend complete understanding of the situation before further action is taken, or forces are dispatched. We do not know who this is, or what it is capable of. This message is an insurance policy, if anything happens to me, this must become top priority. I will continue to report with any relevant information I encounter.

Yours truly,

Zach

I hit send and watched the little rotating circle until the email went through. I knew Michael was probably oblivious to the nature of this situation, though his involvement was more than unlikely, and already beyond his control. I had been assigned to watch him after he was registered, and knew that this situation must be leaving him unstable in some fashion. It was my job to find out more about Jenny and stop her if necessary, keeping Michael in the dark. I did some light investigative work and found out that she would be working the next lunch shift, so that is where I was headed next. Her social media profiles were normal, which they often are.

Having pried up the floorboards for the first time in years, I found my demon kit. It was there in case of emergencies, but I was lucky up to this point that nothing out of the ordinary had occurred. It had the basics as well as a few less common items. I would have to get the holy water refilled, as it had evaporated by this point. There was a small bible, with the 23rd Psalm bookmarked. A piece of white chalk, a small satchel of salt, lighter fluid, matches, a wooden stake, and two relics. One of the relics was a hammer, believed to be used by Margaret of Anitoch. The other relic was a protection emblem that had been passed down from generation to generation in my family. It is believed to stop any fatal attack that may come it's way.

It was Tuesday morning. I stopped by the church on my way to the restaurant to confront Jenny. I wanted to do this during the daytime to minimize incident. At best, she would be agreeable. At worst, we might need a cleanup crew. If things got out of hand I could use the chalk or salt to isolate her movements then finish her off before she attacked anyone else. That was a worst-case scenario. Expect the worst, hope for the best.

Before I walked in, I did a short protection prayer and sprinkled myself with salt. If her reaction to these things was great enough, I would have all the information I needed. I walked into Louie's and approached the host stand. Out of the corner of my eye I could see the tall redhead behind the bar making a bloody mary. It was still early enough to turn my back to her for the brief moment it took to ask the host for a seat at the bar. As I sat down, the redhead handed me menus.

"I'm Zach," I said, holding my hand out.

"Jenny," she replied. It was her. She held out her hand for me to shake, which was the perfect opportunity to see if I felt anything when our hands came in contact. I did. Nothing out of the ordinary though. Just warm flesh.

"I am friends with Michael, is he working today?" I asked, knowing he wasn't.

"He only works nights," she replied. "Do you work with him at the French restaurant?"

"Yes, as a matter of fact, I do. I'm afraid he hasn't said very much about you, how long have you been in town?"

"My family moved here when I was young. I have been working here for three years now, part time. Can I get you anything to drink?" asked Jenny.

"I'll take a virgin Bloody Mary." She went back to making drinks for the rest of the restaurant, then poured half a cup of vodka, topped with Bloody Mary mix for me. I wasn't sure how to read her. She probably knew that alcohol weakens power and perception. I would drink it, but not until I asked at least one more question, one that should be more definitive.

"Tell me," I said. "Have you ever heard of Sanctus Ignis?" Her reaction was normal. Nothing to hide. She hadn't heard of it. It was rare that a full-fledged demon would not know what this meant.

"I'm afraid I don't," she said. "Is it Latin?"

"Yes, it is. It means holy fire. This bloody mary is the perfect color for it. The holy fire is believed to burn away all that is impure with its fiery yellow-orange flames turned to a deep blood-red. It is a beautiful color, I hear, from someone who told me they saw it with their own eyes."

"Wow. That sounds beautiful. Would you like anything to eat."

"Sure. I'll take a hamburger. No cheese. Medium-rare."

"Green Chile okay for you?"

"No. I think I'll take red. It's a much prettier color and it offers greater complexity." She blushed. It was easy. I remembered when I was single and it seemed so complicated. Once you are with a woman for so many years, it is easy to see what makes them happy. Even a stranger can't resistant compliments. As long as they don't have their guard up too high.

"Do you believe in angels and demons?" I asked. She did not react to the question.

"I think one compliments the other. Everything has two sides," she said.

"If you had to be one, which would it be?"

"Neither, actually. I have always sided with vampires. With my skin being so pale, I am practically allergic to sunlight, and I love being out at night."

"Do you drink blood, too?"

"No more than you do," she said, pointing to the drink in front of me. It was tomato juice. Nothing more. She went back to the call bar.

Looking her way, I whispered the words that can't be ignored by an unholy being, "ipsum daemonium revelare." She didn't even glance my way. None of the tests were coming up positive. Hardly a glimmer of anything out of the ordinary. Either I had missed something big, or she was much more powerful than I imagined possible.

The hamburger was enjoyable. I didn't have much else to ask her at this point, so I just continued the meal. The bloody mary was good, they used wasabi to make it spicy. I always believed the best thing to use is Sriracha. I left a good tip for her, she didn't even charge me for the drink. She thanked me and said it was nice to meet me. I replied in kind, still feeling unsure about her.

To: The Association
Subject: Investigation of Unregistered Being

To Whom it May Concern:

I have conducted a preliminary investigation, as mentioned in the last message and the results are less than conclusive. No evidence this person is of our descent or nature. It is clear that something is happening, but as to what and who is involved, there are no leads.

Yours truly,

Zach

To: Zach
Subject: Re: Investigation of Unregistered Being

Thank you for contacting us. Your messages have been noted and registered.
We are taking appropriate action. We recommend you avoid any involved beings and go about your business as usual. There is no further need to make any attempts to contact us.

Formally,

The Association

The last message from the Association was not reassuring. When I contacted them, I was under an entirely different opinion of what was going on in town. Maybe it is better to have backup, but this is close to me and people in my life. I need to take control over it.

I have to find out what is really going on before more people get hurt. It may be time to tell him the truth.

Chapter 13
Kind of Like A Date

It was my first day off in a long time. Work kept me busy. In a good and bad way. I never knew if I would do the right thing with my time off. Today I was doing my best to be good. I woke up early and was eager to make this a productive day. I fed the cat, then put on a facial cleanser that I had made with honey and lemon. After checking my email, I took the time to meditate. I really needed it. I had been feeling very high-strung lately, stressed out about things that I normally wouldn't be. Maybe I was getting too involved at work, or with the other struggles in my life. They weren't important.

Meditation gave me head space to use my thoughts, instead of letting them control me. It went well. I did leg stretches, sang a few kirtan songs, and then did breathing exercises while sitting on the meditation cushion. My mind had a lot to say, but it started to behave halfway through. Silence. Watching thoughts go by. Feeling the energy in and around me. Connecting with it. I later found out that it was a witches moon. Maybe that is why I felt so good that day. I felt so connected for the first time in months. Like I knew myself.

After a long shower, I went to my favorite hangout, a local Spanish tapas restaurant. I sat at the bar and talked with the employees. Some of them had worked with me at other restaurants. This was one of my favorite places to go because they knew me here. On top of that, all of the food was carefully selected. The tastes were all relevant and complimentary. The colors made the dish interesting to look at, but were there for a reason. It was one of the best restaurants in town. Sitting at the bar, I would be closer to being part of the restaurant, instead of a visitor at a table. People were always friendly there. Today was no exception.

This was where I heard a fun song that was in Spanish. My friend later told me that it wasn't very good Spanish. Me gustas tu means I like you. He told me that you can just say me gustas. The tu was irrelevant unless it was referring to another person who was also there. There were a lot of you, me, and it that got dropped in casual conversation. I liked the song anyway, and wanted the chance to say, 'me gustas tu' to someone.

So in walks this girl with dark hair, she is a few inches shorter than I am, wearing an adorable dark blue hoodie, and jeans. She seems like a really cool person. I sat there reading my book. The employees seemed to know her too. She didn't even have money to pay, but they told her she could come back tomorrow. She talks to everyone at the bar and starts to get emotional about something that happened to her earlier that day. She turns her attention to me.

"This guy earlier just assumes these things about me, and it was totally not cool. He doesn't even know me. That's not right, is it?" she asked me.

"No, it seems rather rude," I reply.

"I mean, I don't even know the guy and he just assumes these things about me and who I am." She was being very defensive, insecure. "Anyway, you're cute, what's your name?"

"Michael."

"I'm Sophia," she replies.

"Nice to meet you."

"What are you reading?"

"It's my book, actually. I wrote it. I am reading through to edit it."

"Really? That's awesome. Is it your first book?"

"No, third," I reply.

"Oh, what's it about?"

"It's a love story. Kind of. It's about ego. How it works and how it doesn't. That's the title, A Struggle of Ego. It is about someone who finds that having everything doesn't mean anything."

"That's easy to say when you have everything."

"Experience is the best teacher."

"Do you have everything?" she asked.

"I doubt I would be where I am right now, if I did."

"I know what you mean. Life is always so hectic, things happening that you don't expect."

We talked for a while longer, found out that we were both servers. She said she would have to leave soon to meet up with a few friends to play ping-pong. She said I could come, but that she wasn't going to sleep with me. I thought that was a funny comment, seeing as I hadn't mentioned anything close to that. I agreed. This would be a new adventure. Something to write about in my next book. So I got in her car to go play ping-pong with her friends. A few minutes of driving later, she says she needs to go to her house first, if that is okay with me. It was. She said she wanted me to meet her mom, because she also does reiki.

We go into her house and she introduces me to her mother and her mother's boyfriend. Sophia's cat walks up to me and is very loving. She tells me that the cat only likes her, so that is a sign that I am a good person. I am probably the first nice guy she has ever picked up.

Another woman comes over and tells me that she wants to be a writer as well. I agree to look at her writing one day. We go in the kitchen and find that they are about to eat dinner. Sophia invites me to stay and have dinner with them. She pours me a glass of wine. I sit at the table with her family and listen to them talk about society and what is wrong with it. Her mother's boyfriend has strong opinions about what is right, and thinks he knows everything. I eat my food and nod. Sophia gets upset about it. Soon they end up yelling at each other and I find myself out in front of the house with her and her mother. Her mother tries to console her. She keeps telling me how sorry she is and how awkward it must be for me. Unexpected for sure. She finally calms down when she is alone in the car with me. It is too late to go play ping-pong. We will go to a bar instead. We stop at a gas station and she goes inside for something. We sit outside of the bar in her car drinking out of tiny liquor bottles. It is cheaper than buying drinks inside, and she doesn't have any money. We talk for a while, and she shows me things that are important to her. She does a few freestyle rap songs with an app on her phone. She talks about what it was like in the old days, and how she would rather have lived in the roaring twenties.

We head inside the bar, where she knows everybody. I buy her drinks. I sit at a table while she goes around talking to people. She introduces me to a bunch of strangers, as someone who has written three books. I see hot glowing blue eyes across the room, Jenny, sitting there staring my way. She is alone tonight. Judging me this time. I don't make any attempt to say hello to her, or pick her up. She sits there eerily, staring, watching me. Not even drinking. It is like she just came to gawk. I am a little buzzed at this point, but I am not a very social person. I don't like talking to strangers in bars. Sophia has me watching her stuff while she floats around, the social butterfly she is, looking for some kind of gratification and fulfillment from these lonely desperate souls. None of them attractive. Sophia, Jenny, and I are the only decent looking people in the place. The close second is the dark haired girl with a skrillex haircut, tattoos, and piercings, but she has to be far beyond my threshold for baggage. Though I doubted she was killing anyone. That is just the kind of judgmental mind I had at the time. I decide that I should just leave and give Sophia her stuff back. I look at my watch. It is almost closing time. I have another drink and wait for her to finish talking with everyone, though I don't know for sure if we'll be leaving together. When everyone starts leaving she grabs on to me. She has been doing so all night, flirting in some fashion, I think. That or she is just a physical person. I like feeling her against me. Her energy has potential. She is surprised that I waited for her. So am I. Being the more sober of the two, I drive us back to my place for another drink.

We stand around in my kitchen for a few minutes, taking shots of whatever tequila is left in the cabinet. She says she should get going soon, but instead sits on the couch, fresh drinks on the coffee table. She opens up to me about herself and her life. I listen. I feel bad for her. She is such a pretty girl, she could have everything if she wanted, but wanting wasn't enough. Action was required. I gave her a back rub and we started kissing. I remembered Jenny's words, "remember what happened last time we were on that couch together?" She was a good kisser. Both of them. Though we were drunk at this point. My wrist was feeling tight. The red mala was glowing. My hand seemed like it was becoming a weapon, full of energy. I started to give her a backrub. I loved the way her body felt. Different from Jenny. She wasn't as tall or skinny. She had the kind of body most men desire.

"Do you want to fool around?" Sophia asked me. I took a deep breath, this is what I wanted, wasn't it? There was a thud from inside of the wine fridge. Something struck against it from inside. Sophia didn't notice.

"I really do," I told her, "but I don't think it's a good idea right now."

"You're right. We've both had too much to drink," she said. "I should probably get going. Thanks for having me over."

"Any time. Maybe we can have lunch later this week."

She left. I sat on the floor with my back against the door to the wine fridge. I put my hand to my face, processing everything that was happening. I was so close. I heard another thud from inside of the wine fridge.

"Yeah, I know," I said. Then decided it was time for bed.

Chapter 14

The First Specter

That night while I was sleeping something different happened to me. It was like a dream but much more real. I could somehow sense that it was beyond normal dreaming and reality. I made the decision to keep wearing the relic, the red agate mala, while I was sleeping, and that played a big part in it. I did not yet understand the nuances of its hidden mysteries. I had been buzzed when my head hit the pillow, and after laying there thinking about all that had happened today, my consciousness started to fade. It came back in this unusual fashion that I have been alluding to. Suddenly the effect of the alcohol was gone. I found myself standing in front of what looked like a temple in India. It had glorious carvings of people in all different positions and a great stairway leading up to the entrance. At first I thought no one was there with me. As I walked up the stairs toward the temple, I saw a man with his hands held wide, as if he wanted me to hug him.

"Ah, welcome," he said. "I am so glad to finally meet you."

"Uh, thanks. Who are you again?" I asked him. There was a touch of dream logic inside of this place. I had a feeling like I knew this person but at the same time didn't remember who he was.

"How rude of me. I thought you already knew by now. I guess the storekeeper did not tell you the whole story of this bracelet you are wearing." He pointed to my wrist. When I looked, it did not appear to be the same red mala that it did in the real world, but instead a band that had colors of red and white pulsing through it. The bracelet now appeared to have a life of its own. "I have it too," he said, holding up his wrist, where there was an exact likeness. "We all do. There are three of us, previous owners of this mystical device. In time we will all tell you our story and involvement with the bracelet. It has had many lives, as well, we have, carrying on its message." There were now two other people standing behind this man. "None of us know for sure the origin of the bracelet, but we believe it was created by a mighty being for his own personal use. It is passed on to those who are in need of its powers and lessons. It may seem straightforward, but there is much more to it than you know. You are lucky to have been chosen."

"I don't understand," I said, looking at the bracelet again, this time trying to touch it. My hand went through it, as if it was not really there, but I could still feel its weight on my wrist.

"This is its true form," said the man. "In this world you can see it for what it really looks like. On the lower planes of existence it has many different appearances. It comes to the person in the form that will be most desirable. I still haven't introduced myself! There is so much to discuss, I am sorry. In life I was named Avalokiteshvara, after the son of Lord Shiva, but most people call me Avvy. I am the earliest owner of the bracelet, that we know of. I am sure there were people before me, but we do not know their stories. The power of the bracelet comes from another world that is now separate from us. Are you ready for the first story?"

"Yes, I think so," I replied.

"Excellent. Let us begin."

Thus follows the story Avvy told me of his life:

My story takes place a long time ago in a small village in the heart of Uttar Pradesh. My family was in the lowest social caste of undesirables, but that did not stop us from having a happy and loving family life. My father was in charge of the household, which was the way of society back then. He would always come home looking defeated from a hard day of work and no respect. When he would see his family, his eyes would light up. My sister and I were the most dear to him of all. He never desired anything more than he needed, because he already had everything he wanted in us. Even with the meager amount that he could provide, it was enough for us to have a strong bond for one another.

We went on like this for many years until my sister was old enough to marry. A marriage was arranged, with a man named Rasheed, but as it turns out, this man was of a higher caste. While he did accept the marriage, he wanted nothing to do with our family. He kept her from seeing us and even writing to us. It hurt my father very much to have her so far away from the family. My father would sit outside of her new home after work as often as he could, hoping to catch a glimpse of her.

I tried to console him, and reassure him that she was better off this way and that we had to respect her new life and her husband's wishes. He refused to see it that way. She was his daughter first, and elders were supposed to be respected. It escalated quickly. Rasheed grew very angry at my father's presence outside of his home. He would throw rocks and try to kick the old man as he passed. He told everyone to say nasty things as they walked by my father. When nothing phased him, Rasheed decided there was only one thing left to do. I was there to witness it. He had a group of eight men, two of whom restrained me to make sure I wouldn't cause any trouble. The men punched and kicked my father to death, while Rasheed stood there smirking. I was powerless to stop them. When they finally walked away and let me go, I ran to my father, who was choking out his final breaths. He told me that he loved his family, and that if we could not be together, he would not be able to live in this world anyway. I begged him not to go, but his injuries were too severe. I did not have the power to save him. Never in my life had I felt so helpless. Rasheed just stood there and laughed before going into his house while I kneeled there with my arms around my father.

I went to the authorities, but they said they could do nothing because my father had been on this man's property. It wasn't true, at best he was a few feet from the street. I knew the real reason was social status. What did they care if an undesirable was killed? It just meant less for them to worry about. As far as they were concerned, this man was allowed to kill whomever he wanted, as long as it was someone of a lower caste. I had to watch my mother suffer over the loss, and do my best to console her while they were burning his body by the river. I was supposed to be going to school soon, and she would have no one there with her.

A grave injustice had been committed. My sister did not even make it to her own father's funeral. This was the darkest day for my family. I knew what I had to do. My father could not be remembered like this. I decided I would sit in his place outside of my sister's house, until the time came when Rasheed would do the same to me. I wished there was a way I could do it without suffering the same fate, but I knew it would be the weight on his mind that was true revenge. As I was walking to Rasheed's house to find my seat in my father's place, a man with a goatee bumped into me. He was wearing robes as if he had just come from a temple. I apologized for bumping into him, as he must be of a higher social caste, and it was my responsibility to do so. "Avalokiteshvara," he said, knowing my name. "It is I who am sorry. I know what happened to your father, and you are brave to be walking this path. I admire your courage, but need you to know that real power comes from restraint. Take this as a gift, and don't take it off for anyone. You must sit in your father's place until the time is right. You will know when." He handed me the bracelet that you are getting familiar with. I took it and thanked him for the gift. Anything given to you by a holy man is not to be questioned in my culture, so I took it with grace. I was too set on my path to stop and ask him more.

I put on the bracelet and sat down outside of Rasheed's house, hoping my sister would take notice. At first, I didn't feel anything. I sat there silently, with my legs crossed, waiting, knowing it would only be a matter of time before they beat me too. My sister came out of the house and begged me to leave. She did not want to see any harm come to me. It was then that Rasheed saw what was going on and stormed over to me, furious. That is when I noticed what the bracelet had been doing. I couldn't move a muscle in my body. I was completely frozen. I could not get up from this spot, no matter how hard I tried. I wanted to get up in the man's face and yell at him, but instead I was completely stuck inside of myself, witnessing all that was going on. Rasheed yelled at me and realized that he wasn't getting anywhere. He grabbed me by the elbow, trying to pull me up, but he couldn't get me to budge. Neither could I. There was no force on earth that could move me. He tried to punch and kick me, but I felt nothing. It was like he was hitting a brick wall. Nothing could touch me. I could not even smile at this small victory, though inside I was delighted. It continued on like this. He would try every day as he walked by to attack me in some way, but nothing worked. He called his friends to come and take care of me, but they could do nothing. They tried everything they could think of. They hit me with any object they could find and even tried stabbing me, but nothing worked. My flesh could not be penetrated. I was immovable. Finally, during the night, Rasheed came out to me alone sobbing. "Why must you torment me?" he asked. "I cannot sleep in my own house knowing you are sitting out here like a statue. I am sorry. Your father did not deserve to die. I shouldn't have taken his family away from him. You don't know how people are in my caste. What would they think of me if I associated with an undesirable? I know now that it does not matter what they think. There are greater forces in the world, like that which is binding you to this spot. Please, stand up, get out of this spot. You and your mother are welcome in my house any time you want. I will even take her in, she can live with me now that she has no one. She is a welcome part of my household and so are you, but please, you have to get up from this spot." He was on his knees, begging me. He was a broken man, not through force, but through peace.

With that promise, the full color returned to my face. My head tilted down to look at him and my hand caressed his cheek. Noticing this, he looked up at me with hopefulness, like he had been forgiven. He thanked me and thanked me. When I slowly stood up to my feet, all of my power came back to me a thousand fold. I could feel it burning inside of me. All of the energy that had been withheld from the immobility, and the force of everything they had used to strike me, but my anger was gone now. I had won. I had stood up for my father and showed Rasheed that he could do nothing in the face of what is right. I had all the power I could ever need to destroy anyone, and now I didn't need any of it. All I needed was my family. My mother and I moved into Rasheed's house, but there were some who looked on us with resentment. The servants knew that we were of the same caste as them and looked at us scornfully, though my mother did all she could to help them around the house. Rasheed's friends came by and would look at us with disgust, like we were trash that was festering in the corner. The worst of all was a man named Haleem. I could tell when I looked at him that he had darkness in him.

It made Rasheed very uncomfortable when they would mention it. He did not want to feel weak, and they did not understand why he had made the promise that he did. One night there was commotion in the house. The eight men, under the guidance of Haleem had broken into the house and had grabbed us all from our beds, taking us outside onto the front lawn. Rasheed heard the noise and came running out. He was upset about this, but knew he could not face these men alone. He looked at me helplessly, his eyes asking what he should do. They were going to kill us. Rasheed sat down, in the same fashion that I had, but the first hit in the face from Haleem sent him toppling over. Rasheed had truly learned from his experience, but these men had not. They had just been waiting until the day when they would be able to beat us. Now was their time to see what I was really capable of. The burning inside of me became painful and my hand started glowing a bright red color. My mouth tasted like charcoal. "What are you doing?" Haleem demanded, walking right up to me. I shrugged off the two men that had been holding me back with great ease, sending them falling to the ground on either side of me. Haleem raised his hand to strike me down, but I grabbed his hand before it hit me. My hand was burning into his skin. I held on to it with a death grip. I will never forget the look of horror in his face as his skin started turning to dust. He pulled away from me and held his hand up, staring at it in disbelief. The whole thing started turning into ash and falling away into nothingness. The effect followed his wrist, up his arm and to his body, where it was too late for him to scream. His whole body collapsed into a pile of ashes in the middle of the front yard. Two more of them tried to attack me with weapons and suffered the same fate. The rest of them ran off into the night, while I stood there. What had happened did not make me happy. It wasn't something I enjoyed doing, but it was necessary. They would never bother my family again. Rasheed crawled over to me and touched his head to my feet. I never needed the bracelet again, though I wore it until the day I left that body. With Rasheed's help, we built a statue of my father out in front of the house. My sister visits it every morning, bringing offerings of food and telling him about the previous day.

Power can do all kinds of things, good and bad, it is up to you how to use it, but you must remember that part of your intention will always be left behind on you and your karma. That means if you do good, some good will stick to you. If you do bad, bad will stick to you. Like attracts like. If you continue to go down one path, your life will be unbalanced and you will topple in the direction of your choosing. The bracelet does not discriminate when it comes to using this power. We believe it has already chosen you, knowing exactly what you are going to do with it, and that it is what has to be done for the proper lessons to be learned.

Learn from my experiences that power is just an object like any other. It is only as valuable as the restraint you show. It can be bought and sold, given and received. Its value is only ever as much as your own wanting and desires. This need is mostly in your mind. Once you let go, you can use power for the right reasons. If you drop your desire, you will have no more need for it. So it is a blessing and a curse. You will be lead down a bumpy road with pitfalls on the way. Remember my story when you are in need of direction. There is more to every side than we usually allow ourselves to see, and that only creates more suffering. In that, you must never use power just because you can, but because it is the right thing to do. When it comes down to the point where it is the only thing left to do, then it must be used with restraint and only in the name of what is right.

As Avvy's story wrapped up, the visions of his life disappeared into the soft morning light of my bedroom. That couldn't have just been a dream, I thought to myself, noticing my bracelet looking a little brighter than usual. Would I be able to turn people to dust too? Would I ever want to? I feel like I would get in a lot of trouble for that. I wasn't Jenny, after all.

Chapter 15
Untamed

"Reow," said Ezekiel. He never had an m at the beginning of his calls. I rubbed his head with my thumb, then continued to pace back and forth in my living room. I would have to confront her eventually. I shouldn't feel so weak. The power of the bracelet is more than a match for anything or anyone. It was my own feelings that I was afraid of.

I gently grasped the handle of the wine fridge in my living room, on this faithful morning after the intense dream about Avvy, and pulled. The door opened with a pop, as the seal was broken, letting the cold air out, and the warm air in. She was in there. Sitting in the fetal position. She looked up at me with interest. Those beautiful blue eyes, shadowed by orange-red hair. I lost my breath every time I looked at her. I put my hand out and helped her up and out of the fridge.

"Is it time already?" she asked me.

"Yes. It is. I need your full attention for this," I replied.

"What is it?" she asked, giving my lip a gentle bite. Feeling her so close to me, against my body, was intensely arousing. It made it hard for me to think. I had to pull away to concentrate.

"This isn't working for me," I said.

"What do you mean?"

"This. You here. One minute we are close and the next it's like you don't even know what we have been through. I had a chance to be close with someone else last night, and it couldn't happen because of us, even though you keep making it clear there is no us. Why do you torture me like this?"

"Is it that bad? I thought you liked having me here," she said.

"I do, but I want so much more than you are willing to give."

"I told you to trust me. There are things you don't understand." She held her hands on my face and pulled me toward her, looking directly into her eyes. "I care about you. I really do. I am sorry for what I do, but you have to understand how I feel."

"I don't quite get it," I said. "Either you want this or you don't. Why are we stuck in an in-between?"

"Because that's the way it has to be."

"I can't do it anymore," I said. "I want something that is more... reciprocal."

"I'm giving what I can. What more do you want from me?"

"I want to be closer to you, Jenny!"

"Let's have sex then. You do want to, don't you?"

"Of course, but no, not like this. It would feel too tainted. We would be doing it for all the wrong reasons and it wouldn't solve the real problem here."

"Then what can I do?" she asked.

"I think you should go. I can't have you here like this. Especially when I don't have you. It is a constant reminder of what could be. Seeing you at work all the time is hard enough. I don't need you here in my house with me."

"I'm sorry you feel that way. After all I have done for you. No one else will ever care about you for who you are, and accept what you do to people," she said, walking out the front door. Was it true? Was I really the one who was being emotionally manipulative and abusive? This was not the first time I had been accused of such, but how could I help but feel taken advantage of? I watched her walk by the picture window out front, and remembered her glowing eyes staring in through cupped hands after the bank that day. This is a good thing, I kept trying to tell myself, though I could still smell her scent, and feel her body against mine.

My first thought now was to call Sophia. Total rebound. Not at all what I needed, or even wanted. I didn't love her. I still wanted to be with Jenny. I knew it was hopeless to even think about it. Sophia was closer to my age, anyway, which I think was the real problem with Jenny. Once people have an idea of who you are, it is harder than anything to change their mind. They see age and they qualify you based on it. Then, no matter what, they would rather be with someone based on that vision, even if they love you more.

I made a sandwich for lunch then got ready for work. I would be at Chez Fe that night. At least it would be easy, and there were always good customers.

It was nice working with Zach again. Since they had hired new servers, we had both gotten our shifts cut to accommodate. That is why I had to get the second job. All of this could have been avoided if they just let us do our jobs. I got there first and started detailing the tables. When he walked in the door, I gave him a hug that was longer than a normal one, even though I knew his hands were full.

"How have you been?" I asked him.

"Tired, I have been working all week," he replied.

"Not here though..." I said.

"Yeah, other things. Up at my farm. Lots of work to be done."

"Ah. Yes." A few hours into the shift, Zach brought up what I didn't want to talk about. Jenny.

"I met your friend the other day at Louie's," Zach said. The color must have left my face.

"You did?" I asked.

"Yeah, I went for lunch and she was there. I mentioned that I knew you."

"What did she say?"

"Not a whole lot, but she's not good enough for you. You should stay away from her and wait for someone better. Someone you have more in common with." I knew he was right, but he didn't know how I felt. It hurt to think about it. Especially after I had ended it that morning.

"Well, I said goodbye to her today. We'll still be working together, but I doubt if I will ever see her again outside of work."

"That's good to hear," said Zach. "I was starting to worry about you. You know you can trust me, right? We have been friends long enough that you can tell me anything."

"Yeah, sure. I have told you more than anyone else about what I have been going through, so far."

"Good. I will be here for you if you need me. Don't hesitate to call," he said.

"Even though your phone is always off?" I asked.

"Ha. Yeah. I know I can be hard to reach. I like my space. That's still pretty crazy, what happened last week, isn't it? I mean, getting robbed like that right in the heart of downtown."

"I guess so. No harm came of it."

"Did you file a police report?"

"No. It would be a waste. They don't spend time on things like that," I said.

"You're right. They'll probably get away with it. At least you have your health."

I did have a lot to be thankful for. My job, a roof over my head, my cat, and whatever else money can buy. I guess I even had my health at that point, but I felt like I had lost my sanity. It would be a good idea to go home and meditate, then get some sleep. Would be. I was at another low point mentally. Feeling like the last place I wanted to be was home. I wanted to get lost, to forget myself. After work I walked to the rail station, where there was only one bar. The last resort. Where I had gone with Sophia, and seen Jenny with her ex-boyfriend who she would fuck that night. Why did I want to be there? I didn't, it's just that I didn't want to be anywhere else either. At least I wouldn't know anybody there. I sat at the bar, drinking beer. Their wine list was not good enough for me to touch, but that isn't something that was expected of them. Even the food was mediocre over-priced tavern food, but it was the only thing you could get past ten. I would occasionally look around me to see who had come and gone. It never changed as fast as I wanted it to because they were always the wrong people.

I didn't know anybody this time. Time passed, and the lights started to go up. The bar was closing. It was already two in the morning. Time to walk home. I was a little buzzed, but nothing I couldn't handle. I decided to take the back way home this time. Walking up this dimly lit street with houses, I saw a cat chasing after a mouse in the street. It stopped when I got close, not to give itself up, though I already knew it was there, but didn't run. I doubt if I could catch it, even if I wanted to, but maybe it was friendly. I kept walking and glanced over my shoulder to see the cat trapping the mouse in the middle of the street. It wasn't a very fast mouse.

I walked by a new restaurant that I had been meaning to try. It had already been a year and a half, but initially I had heard bad things from other servers who had worked there. Rumors that they hadn't been paid on time if at all. Recently someone told me that was the old management, and that it was better now. This restaurant was just outside of the radius of places I go for happy hour or dinner. I try to walk less than a mile and a half to get dinner, though I could if I wanted to, just like going to the bar at the rail way.

I took a left, and was walking past some of the government buildings. I lived in the state capitol, which was visible when you were in this part of town, where everything official took place. As I was walking past a cigar shop, I heard muffled noises. There was a black SUV parked in one of the lots a hundred feet back or so. It was shaking. At first I thought someone must be having a good time, but the screams didn't seem like those of pleasure. It seemed like something was happening inside of that vehicle. What could I do? Call the police? They take at least twenty minutes to get downtown from their headquarters, which was ten miles up Cerillos Road. What if I did save this person? Then my name would be in the paper, I really didn't want to draw attention to myself in that way, but what if someone was in trouble? When did that become my responsibility? That had to be the only reason I was put here. I could still feel the energy inside of me, from Jenny, and from the bracelet. I would have to take this chance, it was probably nothing.

Walking up to the SUV, I couldn't see in the windows. Everyone in Santa Fe has to have their windows tinted beyond belief. It's like they actually have something going on in their car that they don't want people to see. I don't buy that kind of crap, except now that I am in this situation and something is clearly happening. I could hear someone screaming inside. Pulling on the handle, nothing happened. It was locked. I pulled back my fist and slammed it on the window. It shook, but was unfazed. The glass is a lot stronger than you would think. I did it again. Still nothing. Then the car door opened. There was a half-naked woman in the back seat. It was clear that she was the one who had been freaking out. I could sense a red darkness in the man's eyes as he stepped out of the car. He had a similar sense as Jenny.

"Oh, brother," the man said, stepping out of the car and looming over me. "Why do you disturb me?"

"You have to stop that," I said to him, as if he was going to listen.

"What business is it of yours?" he asked.

"I can't let you hurt her." With that, he took a step back and started to turn away. It was a trick. He swung his arm at me and sent me flying to the ground. I tried to think of Jenny, to somehow make her come here with me, she was the one who could do something about this. This was no ordinary man. I could feel it. He had to be a demon. His hands started to transform, and his eyes started to glow. Black hair seemed to grow out of him. My heart was racing. I tried to pull energy from the bracelet, to remember what it felt like from Jenny. I needed it. I felt some of it coming and threw my hands forward at him. The hair on his body was gently blown backwards, as if he was hit by a warm breeze. He chuckled, not bothered in the slightest. He stretched his arms, getting his body ready to beat me.

I put my hands behind me on the ground and tried to crab crawl backwards, toward the street, but fell onto something. I reached back to feel what it was that I was sitting on. It was something that had been in my belt buckle. Why was I carrying this around? The gun from the attempted robbery. As this demon man was stepping toward me, I pulled out the gun and pointed it at him. He tilted his head in confusion. I pulled the trigger. There was a loud noise and the creature was visibly struck. He touched the wound and looked at his hand in wonder. Then he struck a fighting pose, both arms out, claws extended, and roared at me. I pulled the trigger again, striking him in the head this time. His body fell limp onto the gravel, with a thump. The girl had already run away. I hid the gun in my coat and ran out of there for a few blocks, then slowed down so I wasn't drawing attention to myself. Someone must have heard the gunshots that close to the plaza, even so late at night. I tried to act natural as I walked back to my apartment, and got there without running into anybody else, having continued to take the backroads.

I got into my apartment and locked the door. Ezekiel came casually strolling out from the hallway. I could smell the recently fired gun. The first thing I thought to do was open the wine fridge. It was empty. Nothing. No wine, no Jenny. Just the refrigeration unit, still humming away to keep the temperature constant. I was still a little buzzed. Maybe that didn't happen. Of course it did. My heartrate was still elevated. I could feel the fight or flight chemicals pumping through my veins. I drank a glass of water. I didn't think I would be able to fall asleep, and wanted to stop thinking about it, so I turned on the TV and watched a few movies. Watched is the wrong word. I let them play in the background, sitting on the couch, while my mind went a thousand miles an hour, thinking about what had happened, and what it would mean. The sun started to come up. Luckily it was my day off.

I would sit at home and recover. It felt like that. A hard come down. Not from the alcohol, I think, but from the intensity of the situation last night, and probably the lack of sleep at this point. I got online and ordered a pizza from the only place that delivers to me. They had a deal for two medium, one topping pizzas. I knew it wasn't healthy, but that wasn't something I should be concerned about. I had already taken a shower, so I knew that I would at least be presentable enough for a delivery driver. Nobody gets dressed up for the delivery driver. It is usually a middle aged man with grey hair, glasses that don't fit his face, and an accent. They always have trouble finding my apartment, because the numbering system was done poorly. It was still morning, but only for another hour. The delivery driver came and went. I sat on my couch, with another movie on, eating the pizza with crushed red pepper. As it got later in the day, I could feel how tired I was getting. I wondered if I would start hallucinating. I hoped it would be Jenny, if I did, or some other girl that would come to me and make me feel better. I didn't really want to be alone, but knew that I should be. It was too soon to talk about this with anyone.

Chapter 16
Stolen Happiness

When I finally crashed into sleep, I found myself having another one of those dreams. Avvy said there would be three. This time the dream started right into the story:

My name is Ramesh, and this is my story. When I was young, my father was a very powerful politician. We were a very well-off family, but I was always a troublemaker. My father thought this would be bad for his reputation, so he had me sent off to live with my uncle in the hills of the Himalayas. After living with my uncle for only a brief time, I became stir crazy, and decided to run away. It became a hard life for me, wandering around, looking for any signs of civilization. At that time there were many miles between villages. I became so desperate, that when I would come across a house, I would take anything of use from them without their permission. In short, I became a professional thief. I became very good at it too. No one would even know I had been there until they were looking for whatever it was I had taken. I was not a greedy man, and tried to take only what I needed, but temptation was too strong sometimes, and I would end up stealing things I couldn't even use. Years went by like this, and I started having a comfortable life because of the wealth I had amassed. I had become out of control. I don't know how people didn't know it was me. I would steal from one town and sell to the next. It was so easy for me to sneak in and out with no problem. My work started becoming legend around town. People were even proud when I took things from them. They saw it as some kind of a blessing. That only made me want to do it more. I became so cocky, and overconfident, but for good reason. No one could touch me.

One day I was walking a different path than normal to get to the small house I was now living in, and I saw a home I had never noticed before. It was right there in plain sight, how could I have missed it? Inside I could see all kinds of valuable things lying around. Pieces of gold and jewels decorating the interior. This was too easy. I had to steal them, and after all, I was doing them a favor by breaking in.

I snuck into the house and was about to pick up a small golden statue, when I heard a voice behind me, and spun around, my heart beating out of my chest.

"Hello, Ramesh," the voice said. It was a man dressed in tattered clothing. I wondered why he would be so poorly dressed, having such riches surrounding him. I couldn't move. I was frozen, staring at him with my eyes wide. I had never been caught before, and in this state of panic, had no idea what to do. "It's okay, Ramesh, you can relax. You don't have to take these things from me, I want you to have them. They are a gift, but you have to do one thing for me."

"What? What do you mean?" I asked him.

"I mean what I say. These are gifts for you. There is no need for you to steal them, you can have them. They are yours, but there is something you must do for me."

"What is that?"

"This bracelet," he said, taking off the only piece of jewelry he had been wearing. I don't know how I didn't notice it earlier, but when he took it off of his wrist, it seemed to be glowing. Surely this must be the most precious thing he had, if he had it so close to himself, but why did he want me to take it? I assumed it was similar to the unburdening that other people felt when I took things from them. You see, we value things for all the wrong reasons. These material things become a burden unto us. It is all things that we have to constantly keep worrying about. I thought surely this man must be crazy, and agreed to take his bracelet and wear it. "There is one catch," the man said. "Having worn this bracelet, you will be filled with awareness. The one thing you have been lacking."

"Awareness?" I asked him. "That is a good thing. I will be even better a thief if I have enhanced senses." I willingly accepted the gifts from this man and quickly put on the bracelet, before leaving with a sack full of his belongings. The next day I went back to see if he would give me any more of his things, but the house was gone. I wonder now if it had ever been there in the first place. Everywhere in town I went, people started admiring the bracelet. It was drawing way too much attention to me.

I would never be able to blend in if I was wearing it, so I decided to take it off. I took the bracelet in my hands and put it in my pocket, but hardly a moment went by when I felt something weighing down my wrist. The bracelet was back. I tried multiple times, even going so far as to hurl it as far away from me as I could, but it came back, brighter than ever. I tried to wrap fabric around it to hide it, but it glowed red through the cloth. It was even more noticeable when I was hiding it. I got desperate and was even thinking of cutting off my arm, but what if that didn't work? Then I would be short an arm and still having this trouble. I became aware of everyone's eyes on me all the time. I could feel myself being watched wherever I went. It made it impossible to steal anything. I would get close to a house and then start shaking, knowing that they were watching me and that I would get caught. I was able to get by on selling the jewels the man had given me, but didn't want to stop stealing. I no longer had a choice. I broke down by the side of the road, crying about the predicament I was in. The bracelet had robbed me of my identity. That is when I was approached by three monks who had been walking this way on a pilgrimage.

"Tell us, what has got you down, sir?" One of the monks asked. The other two had taken a vow of silence, and would not be speaking, but they needed this front man to help them get through society.

"It's this bracelet," I said, holding out my arm. "It has cursed me."

"Oh dear," said the monk. "That certainly does sound like a problem. What is wrong with it?"

"Nothing," I said. "There is nothing wrong with it, it is me. It is too much for me. Everyone wants to look at it all the time. I don't want so much attention on me."

"Why don't you take it off?"

"I have tried, it just comes back, even brighter."

"Have you tried giving it away?"

"No... oh monk, won't you accept this from me as an offering?"

"Certainly. If it will help you, we will take this as an offering." I took off the bracelet and handed it to the monk. He put it on, and the light faded from it. "See?" he asked. "It is not even that special when I wear it. Be free from this curse." They continued walking and I started sobbing, with happiness this time. I held my hands in the air and praised existence. The bracelet was gone. It would no longer plague me with these problems. To celebrate, I would break into the next house I saw along the way. It was a poor looking house, where they probably displayed their riches right out in the open. I was about to climb in the window, when it hit me. Complete realization. Awareness. The bracelet had been a burden to me, in the same way that I was seeing things as a burden to others. It had seemed so valuable to me at first, then became more and more problematic, just like having too much had been. I realized that by taking these burdens, I was the one who ended up carrying them. Everything that I had was a weight on my existence. I didn't really need any of it, and furthermore, I didn't want it. People should hold on to their own burden's, not carry those of others. I had lost sight of my own ideals, and realized that I would always have to carry this weight if this was my lifestyle. The monk had it right. No matter what he had, he wasn't carrying any of it. It was just things. They had no real value. As I walked away from the house, I noticed that the bracelet was back on my wrist again, but this time it was not glowing. It no longer stood out, except to me. Now, I wanted it on my wrist, as a reminder of what I had learned, and it always would be. At first, I wanted to return everything that I had stolen, but realized that it would always be a burden to them, so I collected everything and threw it all into the river. I considered going back to my father, but realized that I had been his burden. Though he loved me, I was a weight on him and his life, as well as the things he desired.

I vowed that I would never lose sight of my own existence. I gained awareness from this bracelet, and it is yours now to experience as well. When there are things in your life that you don't see, it will open the veil for you.

I woke up at eleven the next day. There was something I was missing. Something big. Jenny had a way of finding me wherever I was. At the bank. There in the alley I was walking by. She was in my house, waiting for me. She had gotten there before I could, and the door was still locked. She didn't have a key. Half the time she pretended she didn't know anything I was talking about. Like she was a different person at work and outside of work. I thought that had been her issue. At the bank. It wasn't a coincidence, was it? I walked into my living room, over to the wine fridge. She had been sleeping in the wine fridge. That's what demon's do, isn't it? I opened the door, and found it full of wine. It had never been empty.

"You needed to know," said a voice behind me. I shut the door to the wine fridge and turned around. Jenny was standing behind me. How had she gotten in? She hadn't. She wasn't really here at all. She had been in my head all along.

To: Zach
Subject: Update on Investigation

Zach,

There has been progress on the case you submitted. The body of one of our registered members has been recovered. The case was flagged in the coroner's office when key words triggered our attention. "Extended, claw-like protrusions sticking out from the fingers, probably the result of extreme plastic surgery or birth defect. Feet in similar state. Abnormal bone structure." We took a look into it and sure enough, we were able to identify Ryan Johnson, long-time member and also repeat violator of our terms. There was a witness at the scene who believed she was being attacked. An anonymous passer-by, it seems, pulled the man out of the car and after a brief fight, shot and killed our assailant. The witness fled the scene after the first gunshot. We believe she was going to be his next victim, and that this is indeed the being we have been looking for. Very rarely has there been a case when attacks have been by someone who is not registered. We believe that Ryan was overstepping his bounds without permission to perform these actions. As you are aware, we have support groups to deal with these urges. Here is where the case gets complicated. They also found what they describe as "plus signs" carved into the tips of the bullets, and blood that is a match for an unknown female. As you may know, they were not plus signs, but crosses. We may be dealing with a professional demon hunter.

They have such weapons as these, bullets dipped in the blood of a virgin, and other things from the holy arsenal. Let's just hope they don't have a copy of the handbook, and that this was an isolated incident. I am led to believe that there are one or more demon hunters in your vicinity that are on the lookout for anything suspicious. We don't know if and for how long they were trailing Ryan, but we are surprised they would give up their advantage so easily as this. For the life of one seemingly random civilian. Any known associates, including support groups Ryan may have attended may be at risk, and all registered beings will be sent information on how to protect themselves from unwanted attention. The ground team we deployed has covered up the details of this case, and was able to secure an energy signal to trace. A lot of these would-be demon hunters are only doing it for the power, as you know when a demon is killed, the killer receives his power. Since Ryan was registered, we will be able to scan for his signature and go after those responsible. They have been instructed to investigate and report back to us. Again, we don't know if this is an isolated incident, or a group of fanatics.

Formally,

The Association

Chapter 17

Jenny

"You had to find out eventually," said Jenny.

"It doesn't make sense," I said, reaching my hand out to her arm. I could feel her warm skin in my hand. "I don't get it."

"You need me. You've always needed me. There were things you couldn't do without me, so you brought me here to do them for you."

"What? The things you did... I didn't want that."

"Yes, you did. Deep down, it's what you are. The cross you wear has been holding in your instincts and repressing your needs. This is who you are. You couldn't do these things on your own, so you created me, and used me to do them for you. The man in the alley, the people in the bank, and even the mugging. All of that was just you." She was holding my face again, staring into my eyes to get it through to me that she was telling the truth.

"I can't. I don't. Why would I?"

"Instinct. Michael, look around you. Everyone has been lying to you. They have been telling you who you are your whole life, and it is all a lie. They want you to be something you're not. That's why they gave you this cross to wear. It is to protect them from you, not you from anything else."

Jenny was just a normal person. The real Jenny. She was a single mother with two kids. She had her own life and problems, but not the ones I had imagined. She was just a girl that had rejected me because she didn't know what she wanted. Something had pushed me over the edge. I have always felt like I am not me, but this is not who I thought I was either.

"I hurt those people?" I asked.

"Yes, you did, but it's not your fault. It's your nature. You are a powerful being that has been held back too long. It is time to embrace your nature. Take off the cross and be who you were meant to be. Have your blood and carnage, find peace your way. You deserve to be free."

"No. I don't want to. I like who I am. I don't want to be a monster."

"You don't have a choice. This is who you are inside. If you didn't want it, I wouldn't be here, I would just be another girl you never dated," she said.

She was right. Something inside of me had created this version of her. Why didn't she do things my way then? I had no control over her. I was supposed to believe that was my inner instinct? It was never what I wanted, even if it had been created by my subconscious. I couldn't believe it. I wouldn't. This was not who I was. I wasn't the monster Jenny wanted me to be, and I wasn't the perfect person everyone else did. I was just me. That was what it was. I was trying my best.

I pushed her against the wall and tried to kiss her, but ended up tasting plaster. She wasn't here. She never had been. So I was crazy. I never felt like I was. I thought I had been doing the right things my whole life, yet there was this other side of me that I didn't know about. What did it mean that it was me? What did I think that I was? What makes someone who or what they are? I thought I had the choice. Isn't it my choice?

Chapter 18

Your Son is Special

(Twenty-five years ago, from my father's perspective)

We had our son, Michael, two years before the first real incident. Before that, there were little warning signs, but we thought nothing of it. Things like the stove lighting up too high, which was attributed to faulty machinery, or outlets sparking, which appeared to be faulty wiring. Sometimes we would hear voices in the middle of the night, but we assumed it was part of our groggy dream haze, that none of it was really happening. We didn't know about the in-between states of consciousness, such as the transition from dream to wakefulness, and how they allow you to perceive things on different levels of reality.

My wife had taken him shopping with her that day. He was just a normal baby in the seat of the shopping cart, as she wheeled around the store looking for everything on her list. It was normal until they got out to the parking lot. Everyone in our family likes to park far away from the building, to encourage the extra exercise it takes to walk to the car. Now, this was a very large store, so as you can imagine the parking lot was too. When she got to her car, she was attacked by a crazy man with a gun. He hit her across the face and demanded money from her. I didn't know whether or not to believe her at first, about what had happened, but I could see in her eyes that she was telling me the truth.

Michael, in the shopping cart, just having turned two, looked at the man and spoke to him in a voice that could never have come from a baby. He spoke words we didn't even know, like he knew this other language fluently. There were a number of words he could say, albeit badly, but this was not like that. This was clear and precise, like nothing she had ever heard from a child. "Ubi mors veniet dicitur." We were told that it means, "death will come when called." At his age, he shouldn't know anything like that, most of what he normally said was for food or attention.

My wife swears that his eyes were red at that point, instead of their beautiful dark green. The robber stopped and his hand started shaking, like he couldn't control the gun. He had a panicked look in his eyes as Michael stared him down. The robber put the gun to his temple and called out for forgiveness, before pulling the trigger.

All of this happening in a white suburbanite neighborhood, the police were at the scene almost instantly. They watched the footage on the cameras from the store and called it a suicide, but my wife knew that there was more to it. Something was different about our son. Our family is made up of devout Catholics. My wife was Protestant, before we got married, but my mother insisted that she change her religion before our union. We had even named our son after St. Michael. My wife was relieved that no harm had come to her or our son, but we would have to find out what was going on. First, we took him to the doctor. They said that there was nothing wrong with him. All of the tests they did came out normal, but they did mention power fluctuations on their equipment while they were doing some of the tests. They said this was probably just because of the electric company, but it did happen nonetheless. Second, we took him to the church. They didn't believe it either, but they were willing to baptize and bless him, if it would make us feel better. He screamed the whole time that they did these ceremonies, but they said that was not abnormal. All of this led us to believe that what had happened was some kind of miracle, or gift from God that had saved them that day. With nothing more to do, we continued on with our lives.

Everything was normal for a while longer, and we put him into school. The teachers told us that he had no attention span, and was probably ADD (what is now ADHD). They wanted us to put him on medication, but we refused. We knew from a young age that he had more energy than most children. When we put him down, he would run, but we had been with him long enough to know that he wasn't in need of drugs to make him better. We created a reward system for him and with that in place, and a new teacher, he was actually excelling. He went from the bottom to the top of his class, and everyone loved him.

Later, he got in trouble at school, for fighting one of the other students. The other kid had been picking on him relentlessly, making outrageous claims that he saw our son with claws and horns and blood red eyes. Kids can be so cruel. So one day, Michael hit him, and of course, ended up in the principal's office. They gave him one week of detention, which wasn't very much, because he was such a good student and not known to do such things. That is when the case was flagged by the guidance counselor, who happened to be part of the Association. They ran through our history and assigned one of their men to be of assistance.

A pale, white man with red hair, named Doctor Hamilton. He explained to us that our son was indeed unique. He told us all about demons and other creatures existing on this plane. Frankly, we thought he was nuts, but did allow him to come to our house for a brief consultation with our son. We knew we should let him come because of the incident that had occurred earlier, and we wanted the school to know that we were cooperative.

Doctor Hamilton came to our house a few days later, while Michael was home. When he walked in, he put his head up slightly, as if he was smelling the air for something. He nodded. He walked over to Michael and put his hand on his head, then stood there silently for a moment.

"I'm afraid it is as we thought," Doctor Hamilton said to us.

"What do you mean?" My wife asked.

"Your son is a demon."

"That's outrageous," I yelled at the man, having the nerve to say something like that about our son. He calmly put his hand up and spoke in Latin.

"Ipsum daemonium revelare," said Doctor Hamilton.

My wife and I were completely taken aback, when our sons eyes started glowing red and his fingers turned into claws. What did this mean? That we would have to kill our son? That he was possessed? Michael seemed very disturbed by his own transformation, and slammed his hands into the table. Doctor Hamilton again put his hand on Michael's head and whispered a few words that we didn't hear. Michael took back his normal, beautiful, young boy form.

Doctor Hamilton explained all of it to us. There was no reason that Michael couldn't have a normal life. No one would ever have to know that he was a demon. Nonetheless, he would have a registration number with the Association that oversaw all demon activity. He gave us a cross for Michael to wear, saying it had been owned by a holy saint. It would keep his demon nature from ever coming to the surface. From that point on we always made sure he was wearing the cross. We didn't have any further incidents like the one in the parking lot. He was the perfect son, in fact, he even wanted to be a priest when he grew up. Doctor Hamilton came by a few more times to talk to Michael and to us about how he would be able to live a normal lifestyle. It was hard for us as parents, knowing that our son was a demon, but it was such a misunderstood word. We believed that he was truly our son, and that he would follow our example. We would teach him to be a good person, and that is all he would ever know.

Chapter 19
Vigilante Justice

I wasn't completely sure how to react to the news that I was the one killing people. I still didn't believe it was me, even if it was my subconscious or some sort of demon within me. I thought that the best thing to do would be to carry on life as usual for now, until I could think of something better. It's not like there are a lot of advice sites on this sort of thing. I could find a psychiatrist, but he would probably think I was even crazier than I am. I know bad things have happened, but most of it is true. Isn't it? There are demons. I guess I am one of them. I am not trying to be convinced otherwise, I just don't want to hurt anyone. Now that I know Jenny is in my head, she won't hurt anyone else. Right? I didn't have answers for these questions. I just hoped that knowing was half the battle. That I could stop her now that I knew she wasn't real.

Work at Louie's went by slowly that day. Jenny wasn't there. She had a party to go to and the bar manager was covering her shift. Now that the season was ending, there were half as many customers, and employees. We would only serve five or six tables on nights when there weren't a lot of walk-ins. This was bad for a few reasons, not just the money, but that I was trying to use this as a distraction from my mind. If I was standing around a lot, I would be thinking about my problems more often. I made small talk with the other employees, but it was hard to forget. They say that the best way to solve a difficult problem is to go through the mundane (let your mind rest). I was trying my best, but not getting there. So at the end of the night when I was offered a shot of tequila, I said yes, not considering that being out of my faculties would spur a visit from Jenny. My Jenny.

It worked. I felt a lot more relaxed after that. Looser. It was a cold walk home, but I had my jacket. I knew to put up with being hot while walking there so I could be warm while walking home. The temperature here drops twenty degrees once the sun sets.

As I was opening the door to my apartment, someone called my name. I looked, but did not recognize the man, so I tried to run in, but he pushed me in before I could shut the door. I fell back from the door, onto the floor. Ezekiel, having just walked in, quickly turned and sprinted down the hallway to go hide under the bed. Two other guys rushed in behind the man who had called my name and one of them was now pressing his knee into my back, holding me down. They shut the curtains and locked the door.

"Get him on the couch," the main man said, pointing. The two bigger men, presumably muscle, were dressed in black suits. The one who had been doing the talking had a style of his own. He was wearing a fedora and a trench coat. He had thin, wireframe glasses. The two men searched me and took away anything that I had on my person. To my objection, they took off my cross, bracelet, and of course, the gun I had in my waistband. They sat me down on the couch, then stood nearby. The main man picked up the gun and emptied it out, holding up the bullets and smiling.

"Yep, you're the right guy. Now, you're going to answer a few questions for us," said the main man, "and don't try anything stupid." He motioned toward his associates, who pulled back their jacket's briefly to reveal guns.

"Who are you?" I asked.

"We work for the Association," said the man. "You probably don't know about us. When things go wrong, we pick up the pieces. They send us to go after scum like you." I kept my mouth shut. I wasn't going to confirm or deny that, until I heard what they meant. "You don't seem surprised, about us being here. That means we have the right guy. We are what you might call the cleanup crew. When things get out of hand, we come in to take care of them. You must agree, things have gotten pretty messy. Usually we spend more time investigating and bring offenders to the Association, but in cases like yours, we make exceptions. The case will go cold, after we dispose of your sorry little demon killing ass. We traced the energy signature of your last victim, and erased any trace of it, so no one is going to come looking for you."

"It was an accident," I said. "He was attacking that girl." They were telling me way too much. I knew I didn't have much of a chance of leaving this room.

One of the muscle men spoke up for the first time, "That is what the police report said." The main man just pointed a finger at him and didn't say anything. The muscle man stop talking.

"Start talking," said the main man to me.

"I will tell you everything," I replied. "But you have to give me my cross back first."

"Ha. It's not going to protect you from us. We're not demons. We are just employed by them. Start talking."

"You have to give it back to me first!" I said, louder this time.

"No!" he yelled, slamming his hands on the coffee table. "Tell us what we need to know."

"Okay." I said. There was no use arguing the point any further. "I was walking back from this bar at the rail way, and heard muffled screams coming from a car, so I got closer. That's when this big guy gets out and starts going demon on me. I'm not very strong, so I shot him. All the while, the girl kept screaming in the car, but she ran away before I could talk to her. He was attacking her. It was self-defense, I swear." The main man paced back and forth, listening to my story.

"And you just so happened to have demon slaying bullets in your gun? By coincidence? Are you going to tell me that?"

"What? No. I don't know. It's not my gun."

"That's enough. I didn't come here to be lied to." The muscle guy on the right stepped over and hit me across the face, then stepped back. I felt my head spinning, the guy was strong, then pulled myself back up to a sitting position. My body was getting hot. My heart burned. The energy was coming. There was no cross to stop it. The bracelet was back on my wrist.

"Please," I said. "You're making a mistake."

"You're in no position to tell us what we're doing, little demon-slayer."

"I'm not a demon slayer, I'm a demon."

"Ha. Yeah, right. Demons don't kill their own kind on a whim. If you're a demon, what is your registration number with the Association?"

"I don't know. I don't think I am registered. I didn't know until recently."

"Bullshit." The muscle guy on the right came over and hit me again, this time I tried to hold my arm up to block him, but it didn't make a difference. I fell to the floor in front of the couch on my hands and knees.

"Now you're going to tell us about your friends," said the main man, holding his gun against my head. "You have to say something useful before you die."

THUD

On my hands and knees, I was facing the floor. There had been a hard thud in front of me. Fear ran through my body. Something was coming. I looked up. It was the wine fridge. The others were staring at it as well.

THUD

"What was that?" One of the muscle guys asked.

"There's something in that cabinet," said the other one.

"What's in the cabinet?" The main man yelled at me.

"Go!" I yelled back. "You have to get out of here."

"We're not going anywhere."

THUD

"What's in the cabinet?" The muscle guy said in a scared whiney voice starting to freak out. He was right to. I had to tell them.

"My ex-girlfriend," I said, standing upright, feeling her taking over.

The door to the wine fridge burst open, hitting one of the muscle guys so hard he was sent flying back against the door of the apartment. I heard gunshots and screaming. Jenny had the other muscle guy up against the wall, holding him by the neck. She looked directly at me, grinning, and shoved the claws of her other hand into his neck, pulling them downward, slicing easily through his bones. She brushed him aside and flew over to the other like a bird. Screaming. Gunshots. She was ripping into his neck with her teeth, her head going up and down, pulling out whatever she could get between them. My carpet was changing color into pools of dark red.

"What the fuck," the main man started to say, firing his gun at her, but she just walked through the bullets. They were using normal bullets, presumably for normal humans. Demon hunter hunters. They were not prepared for this. That is why the Association wanted them to investigate, not take action. They didn't know what they were up against. I listened to his inhuman screams as Jenny took her time with this one. She slowly pushed a single claw into his shoulder, as she held him in the air by his neck.

"You should have listened to him," she said. She pulled out the claw then lifted it higher, to his face.

"No, please don't," he said. "It was all a mistake. I'm sorry!" There was no forgiveness in her. She pushed the claw through his glasses, into his eye, deeper, into his brain, all the way in, then let him fall limp to the ground. She walked over to me and pushed me on the couch, then got on top of me. I could feel the blood on her hands that was now on the sides of my face. She kissed me. Those warm lips. Her soft tongue. What she had just done. Bodies littered the living room floor. She licked my face, making it sticky from the blood in her mouth. Yummy. I want her so badly. I feel so close. I shut my eyes. Take me away Jenny. I miss you so much.

"We need to do this more often," she said, smiling at me with her now beautiful blue eyes and a giggle. This was the happiest I had seen her in a long time. She got up and stepped into the wine fridge, shutting the door behind her. I sat there in shock and awe. I looked down and saw a bullet hole in my right shoulder quickly heal itself. The energy was rushing through me. I walked over to the bodies, and put my hands on each of them, remembering Avvy's story. The bracelet glowed, and each of their bodies was turned to dust. The blood went along with them, except for a few splatters here and there, that were too far away. I would have to clean those with bleach and a towel. Good thing I had rug cleaner. Thank God this worked.

The smell of raw meat lingered on my clothing. I put my clothes into the washer and got in the shower. I watched a spider struggling to keep up with the current, but inevitably, it was carried down the drain. It interested me that bugs could drown. They are so small. It must have seemed like a giant flood. People die that way too though. All over the world, floods and mudslides. We are just as small as that spider. Do we have the same thoughts as we are being carried down the drain?

Chapter 20
The Lost Truth

"Zach, I have to talk to you about what happened yesterday," was the first thing I said, when I saw him at work the next day.

"What is it?" he asked.

"I am a demon," I said.

"You finally found out?"

"What? You knew?"

"Michael. You and I are both demons. That's what I meant when I asked if your friend is like us. I thought you knew."

"What? How long?" I asked.

"I have been part of your life on and off since you were a child. I was the one assigned to protect you, that is why we are working together now. Do you remember seeing me as a child? I haven't changed that much." I didn't remember anything like that. "Does the name, Doctor Hamilton ring any bells? That is the name I went by. I was your therapist for a short amount of time, but mostly watched from afar." The name was familiar. I did have a therapist with that name, but I didn't remember anything about him until now.

"That was you?" I asked.

"It was, yes. It's okay. Don't worry. There is nothing wrong with being a demon in this day and age, but now that you know, there is a lot we need to talk about. How did you find out?"

"Jenny. She wasn't real. She was in my head. I mean, there is a real her, but she wasn't the one I was seeing. It was something inside of me."

"Shit! I missed it. Your demon essence was trying to escape, and it used her as a back door so to speak. Now that you know, it shouldn't happen anymore. Don't be afraid. You are in control."

"I know, but those things that happened. I didn't mean for them to happen. I can't help but feel responsible."

"I should have been watching you closer. I thought it really was the girl you mentioned, until I met her in person. She is just a normal girl. Your mind was playing tricks on you."

"I know. I believe it all now. Everything makes sense, even though it doesn't. How could this happen? I don't understand any of it. I didn't even think demons were real a few weeks ago."

"They are real. It would take too much time to go into the history of it right now. We will talk about that later. We need to get through this shift, then I will come with you to explain where we go from here."

"This is such a relief. I was afraid you were going to freak out. You are the only one I feel like I can talk to about any of this."

"That's right. I am here for you, and you have to keep the rest of this a secret. Anyone that knows is in danger. The Association does not like loose ends."

"Association?"

"Yes. There is a large organization of beings like us. They monitor our activity to make sure we are not getting in any trouble, or being chased after by anyone else. We have kept our existence secret this long, and it has to stay that way. Every demon is registered with the Association, including you, when they are born and identified. From there, they are given a sponsor, someone like me to guide them and make sure they make the right choices in life. Everyone has a right to live, including demons, but they cannot affect quality of life for others."

"I see. When am I going to meet these people?"

"That doesn't happen. They contact you remotely. I have only met one representative in my whole life."

After work that night, Zach gave me a ride home and came in with me. I opened a bottle of wine for us to drink, while he continued to tell me about demonhood.

"Where to start," Zach said, sitting next to me on the couch. "As you know, there are demons among us, and we are both in the same boat. Demons have a choice of being good or bad, but don't often exercise that freedom of choice. We live in a world now where mischief and mayhem are not the only things that make the world go round for us. You are either born a demon, or you're not. Most of the time one of your parents is a demon, but every so often, the demon energy wants to come to earth, and uses a willing couple to do so through childbirth. The woman acts as a gateway." This sounded like the sex speech my dad gave me when I was thirteen.

"I think we can skip this kind of stuff," I said.

"Sorry. Biology is really interesting to me. The miracle of life, and all. It really is amazing how it works. You have been a demon since birth. There are stories about people being possessed by demons, but mostly they were just unidentified demons whose energy flairs, showing a completely different personality in what they thought was a normal child. In short, you either are a demon, or you're not. There is no in between. Here we are. Both demons. It's not just us. That is what I really wanted to talk to you about. There are many like us all over the world. Furthermore, there is a support group for us. It is a group where demons can feel safe talking to each other about their urges, crashes, and everything like that without feeling judged. We have all been there. Would you come to a meeting with me?"

"Sure. I would love advice on dealing with this energy inside of me. That's what I wanted to talk to you about. There was a group of men here yesterday. They thought I was a demon hunter and wanted to torture and kill me. They had traced me from a demon that I killed, and destroyed all of the evidence so that they could take their revenge on me."

"They did? Seriously? What happened?"

"Let me tell you the whole story. The other night when you interrupted those two thugs from mugging me, I got his gun before they got away. A few nights later, I was walking home from a bar at the rail station late at night, and I heard these noises coming from a black SUV. I knocked on the door, and out steps this massive guy, who I can tell is a demon. His form is exactly what I have seen in the past, sharp claws, glowing blood red eyes, you know what I mean. So I try to fight him, but I am obviously no match. That's when I realize that I still have the gun. I shoot him in the gut, then in the head, and it works. It kills him. I figure it's normal, that we're just not bulletproof. As you know, that's wrong. So these three guys follow me home the next day and push me into my apartment. They sit me down on the couch and show me that the bullets had crosses on them, that they were made for killing demons. They think I am a demon hunter. They don't give me a chance to explain any of it. They took everything I had on me, including my cross and laid it out on the coffee table. I told them I needed it, but they laughed, not knowing I was a demon. As they started to hit me, I fell to the floor and Jenny came out. Out from inside my mind. I watched her tear them apart, all of them, like it was nothing. I know now that it was me, but it was self-defense. I wish they had just talked to me instead. They dug their own graves." Zach looked at me, nodding, his hand on his chin. He lifted his glass of wine and took a sip.

"Ha!" he said, with a laugh. That's what they get for not listening to the Association. I heard there was going to be people investigating, but had no idea it was you at the time. You're in the clear. They are looking for real demon hunters, not registered demons like you, and if those guys got rid of the traces so that they could have you to themselves, they got what they deserved, and no one has any clue. The reports all blame the demon you killed for the recent deaths and attacks. In short, you don't have to worry about anything. You are off the hook."

"That's great, I think. Though I still wish that none of this happened in the first place."

"It couldn't have worked out better. Everything happens for a reason. The only concern now is those thugs. If they really are demon hunters, we need to find out what they know about us, and you. It was no accident that they encountered you in the alley that night. They knew exactly what they were doing, but underestimated you."

"I only wonder one thing, when they shot at me with the demon killing bullets, I caught one of them. How is that possible?"

"It's not unusual for us to be able to do things like that, but with those demon slayer bullets, that is a good question. The only answer I have, is that you had your cross on at the time. The energy you were using was escaping from around it, not what was defining you. You must have been riding a very thin line between catching it and having it kill you. You are lucky. As far as the investigation, it seems that the trail has just gone cold. They may keep trying to find demon hunters in the area, but without that energy signature, no one will be looking for you. All the more reason that you need to come with me to a meeting as soon as possible. We need to make sure you stay in control of what is inside you."

"I'm all for it," I said. It was quite a relief. A lot of things I didn't even know about, all working out somehow. Someone must have been watching over me. I made plans with Zach to go to the meeting on the only day off we have together, next Tuesday. I was glad it was a few days away because I needed to think about all of this. I needed time to process it.

Chapter 21

Demons Anonymous

I postponed thinking about it as long as I could, but Zach was at my front door, and I would have to go to the meeting with him. It isn't that I didn't want to go, I was just nervous. This would be the first time I was around other demons. That wasn't fair though, was it? They were just normal people like me, and that is how they wanted to be seen. It's bad enough that outsiders look at them differently, it wouldn't be very pleasant if the insiders did too. I can't even imagine the things these demons had done though. They probably didn't know about my secrets either. Were they all as helpless to control it as I was? Somehow I felt like I had been kept in the dark longer than others. If I had been allowed to embrace this as a child, maybe I would have been in control of it from the very start, or at least only had minor incidents, not involving people, banks, and Jenny.

I wondered how often Zach went to these meetings. He seemed to be very in control of himself. Not many people were like that. Including me. Even outside of the demon spectrum, I was one for indulgence when it was presented to me, albeit that was not as often as I would have liked. Sometimes I was led to believe that fear was a motivator for him, he did not like to take risks. Everything he did was calculated, with precision. If you want to be around as long as he has, that is the only way. I wondered if there was any passionate part of him that would fight if it came down to it. I am sure he would for himself, and probably even his family, but was I a good enough friend for that? The question also arises, would I do that for him? In what context?

We arrived at the Presbyterian church that holds these sort of meetings. This was surprising to me. A bunch of demons meeting at a holy place.

"A church? We're not going to burn up or anything when we walk in are we?" I asked Zach.

"Ha ha. You've been watching to many movies. This is a neutral meeting ground for all beings. A safe place for everyone. In demon form, it may not be the most comfortable place to be, but we are coming here as people who know they need help, not as demons," Zach replied.

There were other people walking in the side doors before us, probably for the same thing. There was a guard at the entrance, which was a strange thing to see at a church. They needed to make sure that everyone who entered was a demon. This was not open to humans.

"Can I help you?" The doorman asked us.

"We're here for the meeting. It's okay, we're both registered," Zach said. The man looked us up and down and stared at each of us individually, as if he could see into our souls. He let us in.

As we walked through the doors, I asked Zach, "How does he know if we're demons or not?"

"He has the sight," Zach replied. "Every demon has different powers, some of them can see energy. There are rumors that all of the powers are attainable to every demon, but that it takes a certain kind of practice and willpower, as well as peace of mind, to attain them. Being able to see energy is one of them."

"What would he do if we were human?"

"He would kill us on the spot," Zach replied.

"Really?"

"No, not really. He would just tell them it's a closed meeting. Give us some credit."

"Oh," I replied. That wasn't funny. I didn't know anything about what they did. There was a meeting hall, in the recesses of the church itself, in the back. There were a few tables that had been placed in a U shape so that everyone could sit in something like a circle. It was supposed to make it friendlier. When you first walked in there was coffee and snacks right after a kitchen, then the full meeting space. I poured myself a cup of coffee. The meeting was getting started. There were all kinds of interesting looking people around the room. Most of them looked like they were about to die. These were other demons. I expected them to be strong and powerful, yet here were these weak and fragile looking people. Being a demon was destroying their lives, and they came here for help. It was the first time I questioned whether or not I really should be there. I didn't feel like I had hit rock bottom just yet. Could these demons heal themselves if they went into demon form? Why wouldn't they? Just for a few hours, at least. It would make their lives better, and make them feel better.

There was a picture of a man that I recognized at the front of the room, with flowers around it. It was a memorial. For the demon I killed. If only they knew it was me. There was an emaciated looking man leading the meeting. He was tall and boney. He had short brown hair and was wearing brown pants and a white t-shirt that was too big for him.

"Before we get started," he said. "We are going to take a few minutes to remember Ryan." He pointed to the photograph. "Ryan had been coming to us on and off for a few years, and this is one of the sad stories that comes from relapse. He wasn't perfect, none of us are, and I like to think that we did all that we could to be there for Ryan. He did not use his resources to try to contact any of us before he went on this rampage that ended with him being shot and killed by a demon-hunter. This is one of the main reasons for our anonymity. It is very important that no one knows who we are and what we are, because they judge us unfairly. I will not try to justify what Ryan did and what happened to him because of it. I just want to remind you that this only works if you use it. We are here for you, but you need to come to us when you need help. We can't help anyone that doesn't ask for help or doesn't want it. I know you are all here because you know the severity of this problem that we share. I know you are here because you want to get better. We all want to live normal lives and be successful in our endeavors, but that fact does not change what we are. There is something inside of us, and it is a powerful force to be reckoned with. Coming to these meetings will help you control it, and will help you understand yourself. We can use this as a gift or as a curse, but either way, we need to know what we are up against, and how to be in control. Please join me in a moment of silence for Ryan."

We sat there in silence. Some people cried. Some covered their faces. Everyone here knew him. Everyone except me, the one who killed him. I had never taken the time to think about it. He had a whole life as a normal person, outside of that attack. That could have been me. Did he deserve to die for it? It felt like a wrong person at the right time moment. Me, another demon, conveniently walking by at two in the morning, carrying a demon hunter's gun. What are the odds?

I could see there were other people that were impacted by his death. He wasn't just a monster. We all have more than one face, and no one is ever truly innocent, or guilty.

"I know there are some new faces today, so I would like to take time for everyone to introduce themselves. I am Sam, I have been leading the Tuesday group for three years, and have been without incident for over twelve, thanks to the help of this group. I also want to mention that if this is your first time, it is okay if you don't want to participate. Everyone moves at their own pace, the important part is that you are here and know that we can help you if you are willing to ask for help." One by one, they stood up, going around the table, telling their names.

"I'm Julie. I have been clean for two years."

"Ella. I transferred from the Thursday group because of my schedule, so this is my first meeting here, but I have been to others for seven months." After each person spoke, the crowd clapped gently, slightly more than a golf clap.

"Edward, this is my first meeting."

"Johnathan, I was ordered to come here by the Association. I don't think I really need to be here."

Everyone nodded, looking at the face of denial. They could tell who would last and who wouldn't. The first step was to admit you had a problem. That usually came with coming of your own free will. Edward and Johnathan didn't look like they wanted to be there. They would probably suffer the same fate as Ryan, but not at my hand. There were demon hunters here, they had even found me. I had misbehaved.

"Simon, I have been coming for two years now."

"Zach, I have been coming on and off for forty years." Everyone clapped a little louder for him. Most of the demons here were young. They didn't know anyone beyond their own generation. Most of them kept to themselves, including Zach, who was here today for me.

"Michael," I said, standing up. "This is my first meeting."

"Cleo, this if my fourth meeting."

"Mark. I have been coming for three years."

"Thank you to everyone for coming," said Sam. "If there are no objections, I will tell my story today." Nobody said anything. Someone took a sip of coffee on the other side of the room. Another person kept sniffing their nose. "I was in college when I found out that I was a demon. It was while I had my first girlfriend. Yeah. You can see where this is going. I wish I had. Everything was going well, until we took it to the bedroom. That's when the elevated state of excitement took me out of my body, and brought out my demon form. I never heard from her again after that night, but I didn't hurt her. What happened was strange and confusing to me, and I thought that I would have to deal with it on my own. I thought that it was my burden to carry, and that I would be able to control it. I was wrong. This was before I knew anything about the group and meetings. Everything was great for a while, then animals around campus started disappearing. It turned out I was going demon at night, while I slept, and eating them. Then came the powers. I could light things on fire with my mind. It was more than useful in getting out of boring classes. Eventually someone noticed what was happening, and I found myself dealing with the police, being accused of arson. That is when I was contacted by the Association. They explained everything and taught me how I should be living. From then on, I knew I needed to be around people like me. For encouragement and support. No one else could understand what I was going through. That is when I started coming to the meetings. I am Sam, and it's been twelve years since I hurt anyone. I hope those of you who are new can especially learn from my story. There is help available to you. You just have to ask for it."

Everyone clapped. It didn't seem like a really big deal to me. I had killed people. He had just lit things on fire. Sam continued the meeting by reading from a book and talking about the different rules they had in place. When the meeting was dismissed everybody got up and mingled. Zach introduced me to other members and I got a few phone numbers of people to call if I was in an emergency. Some of them wanted to hear more about Zach, but he shrugged them off onto what he wanted, which was to stay private. One thing I learned from the meeting was that I did not want to be like these people. They were afraid of who they were. They were so helpless. Was that what I had become? I didn't feel like I was in control, but I wanted to think that I could be. In time. That I had a choice. I was brought up to always be responsible for my actions.

"What do you think?" Zach asked me, as we drove back to my apartment.

"Nice," I said. "I mean, it's nice that there are people to talk to. People like me. I think I need to go more often."

"I'm glad to hear you say that. I'm happy to take you any time. The first step is knowing you have a problem. We can beat this together."

Chapter 22

Chaos

I kept going back into my bedroom closet to sniff the panties I had stolen off her floor this morning. I would be lying if I said that is all I was doing when I smelled them. It was barely after noon, and I had already done it twice. Not to mention the three hours this morning actually with her. What is wrong with me? It was carnal. Lust. I wonder if it will happen again. It was my first time with a demon. Like that, I mean.

Do you even remember her name? Of course I do. I like her name with a y, but she likes it better with an a at the end. Had I betrayed Jenny? No. There was no Jenny. The real Jenny had her chance with me. I wanted her to see me happy, for once, especially knowing that it could have been her getting all this special treatment. I wanted to make her jealous.

We had exchanged numbers after one of the meetings. This is what they call the thirteenth step. Ella was an attractive, older woman who would frequently speak in the meetings. She had been dealing with the same things I had. There is a mutual understanding between people who are going through the same thing. I think it has to do with empathy. They are the only ones who really know what it's like. They are the only ones who can truly understand. Her face was an upside-down triangle that accentuated her cheekbones. Her dark hair had been well kept, though I would later find it messy when she let it down. Her eyeliner was a thick black that conveyed a darkness in her that I knew was there. She wore bright red lipstick and black-rimmed glasses. Ella looked like a librarian. I still wanted to call her Elly, but I understood the difference. She had at least seven tattoos, none of which were visible. All of which I would see that night and in the morning while she slept through her alarm and I continued to explore her body.

Beautiful butterflies, flying over her shoulder blade. A hummingbird fluttered halfway down her back, near the middle, but to the left side. I think she secretly wanted to fly away from all of this. There were a lot of winged creatures on her back. I always wanted angel wings. I'm not even sure why. I have always seen myself as a fallen angel. That wasn't too far off, it seems. Demons must have come from somewhere. The question came, if angels can fall from grace, can demons rise up to it? Could I live a normal life? I didn't even *feel* normal anymore. Then again, I didn't before either. This just solidified it.

Ellybear called me because she needed someone to talk to. That was what she had said, at least. We met up at a local hotel-bar, that was going to be opened for at least one more hour. I got there first. Ordered a glass of cabernet. Schmoozed with the bartender, who I used to work with. He gave me a discount. Being nice to people pays off. She sat down across from me. I am not too loud of a talker. I told her she should come sit next to me instead. She agreed because she can't hear very well. Not a good start. She went to the bar and got a glass of wine. We were sitting next to a nice little fireplace, that had a fire going, but fake wood. It was still nice.

We built rapport over shared experiences with the same guru. She had his pictures on her wall. I had them on my altar. She was using me for answers. Not intentionally. She needed them, and had created me to give them. Someone outside of her life. They told us the bar was closing, but that there was a side room we could sit in as long as we wanted. I had seen a security guard sleeping on a couch when I walked to the bathroom earlier. Ella thought that was hilarious. Mostly because he did come to kick us out eventually, and we should have said, "Go back to sleep and let us sit here." The side room was very nice. There were beautiful classical paintings around a table, and a second, deeper room that we sat in. In this smaller room, there were temperature controlled wine-refrigerators. I had to try the handle. They were locked. Too much temptation. It was probably their reserve wine.

We had a long conversation about being able to help people. She was a social worker during the day and had to deal with a lot of things that most people would never dream of. I never asked for details but was given some about the horrible smells and poor lifestyle choices. It sucks that you can't help people who really need it. They are the ones not willing to change. She was very adamant that some of their lives were hard and they kept getting setbacks. I told her that the most important thing was how they looked at it, not how we did. A setback is an obstacle that needs to be overcome. Fair or not, teach people to deal with problems instead of to surrender to them. If they complained about these things and didn't try to get past them, it was a wasted effort to feel bad for them.

This was a harsh reality that I was laying on her. It wasn't up to us. I feel like a lot of problems in life revolve around lack of education, but even the educated make poor choices. It had to be our karma that we were trapped in. Our life. The way it had to be. It was hard to look at and see people suffering, but it was their suffering to carry. The most compassionate thing to do would be to listen. That's what they needed most. Someone to hear them. That is what eases the pain. Someone to make them feel heard, and understood. It would make them feel better than any real solution. Of course, the moment they asked for help and were ready for it, you should be there to offer. If they aren't ready for it, it will fall upon deaf ears. You can't take people out of their suffering. All of this explanation of how the world works was coming out through me and I couldn't help but wonder. What was our suffering? What was my suffering? Being a demon? Having Jenny kill through me? My attachment to her. That's what it always came down to. How could I still be thinking of Jenny?

I went to another bar with Ella, but soon after it was last call there too. We stopped by my house for a bottle of wine, then went back to her place. It would be nice to hold someone in my arms tonight, I thought. To wake up next to a pretty girl. I sat on her couch and opened the wine with a wine key that I brought with me. She handed one to me, oblivious. We had already had a lot to drink. I didn't want any more, but she asked me to open it. She drank it straight from the bottle. Her thirty pound cat watched us from the corner. That had to be the fattest cat I had ever seen. Impressive. I didn't like his energy. She told me that the cat was her familiar. That all demons have one. "We are attracted to each other," she said. I thought that Ezekiel must be my familiar. He was orange, after all, and I had such an affinity for anyone with that color hair.

It was already past three in the morning. She said she had to get up early. Another time she told me that she never slept well. How did she expect to when it was only going to be for a short amount of time? We weren't going to be getting a lot of sleep for the next few hours, as it turns out. I took my pants off and got in the bed while she choose some animated cartoon to put on TV. We talked about the TV shows that we both liked. She showed me the pictures of the guru on her wall. It was amazing that we both followed the same one. She told me that she had only been going to the meetings for a few weeks, just like me, and that I was the first one she reached out to.

"I don't know exactly what I am looking for," Ella said. "I don't have a lot of free time and I guess I just want someone to sleep with. You know? Casual sex."

"Do you want to have sex?" I asked. "Turn around." She had been facing the TV, away from me. She turned around. We kissed. Then felt each other's bodies. We took off our clothes and you can guess what happened from there. Neither of us entered demon form while we were intimate. I had been hoping we would, but didn't think I could be in control if it happened. I held her in my arms all night. We didn't go to sleep until five thirty. She had to be at work at nine. I had to put my underwear back on because there was no way I was going to be able to stop ending up inside of her if I didn't. My hands were all over her body any time I was awake. After pressing the snooze button three times I got up and put my clothes on.

I was freezing. It couldn't have been that cold. I think I was just hungover that badly, or possibly from the lack of sleep. I was shivering. I got back under the covers. I didn't guess how long she would be staying in bed. It would have been nice to have the whole day off to cuddle. I was lying on my back, under the covers next to her, clothes on, and the cat jumped up onto the nightstand to get onto the bed. I doubted the cat could jump as high as the bed. He walked over and sat on my chest, face right in mine. I could feel his claws in my throat. Was he threatening me? He kept pushing his head against me. I rubbed the side of his face. It was freaking me out, seeing that cat face so close to me. The thing was as big as a lion. I turned over slowly, so that the cat was finally in between Ella and I. I still wanted to touch her. I laid on top of her and eventually got enough room on the other side of her, to wrap my arms around her again. I nibbled on her shoulder and back, gently. She wanted to sleep. I wanted to play. Finally getting up for work an hour late, she drove me home. "I'll call you," she said, as if it had been a job interview. Don't call us, we'll call you. I had pushed too hard for a second meeting. Sex would be better sober. I decided I wouldn't send her anything, and instead, wait and see if she was true to her word.

It didn't matter. It was only a friends with benefits thing. Not even friends. I had already met someone else that I cared about. Someone who felt like they had been in my life forever. Like we knew each other in a past life. We would be going on a date the next day. I hoped it would go well.

Chapter 23
The Next Redhead

She was a wannabe. Though I didn't know that yet. The next girl. I met her online. I had looked for girls online in the past, but it was never successful. Everyone seemed to be crazy. Seriously fucking crazy. I have heard that about the guys too, not just the girls. You can't meet normal people online. Normal isn't exactly what I was looking for, just people I could have a connection with. I had been talking to Lilith for two weeks already, a record in the online dating community. We had already exchanged social media profiles, and phone numbers. We sent each other pictures every day and talked about life. By the time our date arrived, I already knew most of her likes and dislikes. I had bought prosecco and the type of chocolates she liked. I was going to bring the chocolates, but forgot them when the time came.

I stopped by Louie's on the way, to pick up my paycheck from the previous Monday. It was Wednesday. My only day off. That was why I picked it for the date. By chance, Jenny was bartending. She told me that she had picked up the shift for someone else. On top of that, one of my ex-girlfriends was at the bar. I gave out hugs to everyone that knew me. I told them I was going on a date. I kind of wanted them to be jealous. They should be. They had missed out, though the one currently drinking at the bar had not stopped seeing me by choice. Not her choice, I mean. I hadn't called her back after spending a drunken night at her house. She was a nice person, but just not the one for me. I hoped there was no bad blood between us. It all still felt so fresh with Jenny, even though two months had passed at this point. I knew she still liked me. The real her, I mean. Not the one that was in my head. I could see conflict in her. Other times she was too preoccupied with herself to care. I took the check and thanked her then headed out to the Italian restaurant where I would be meeting Lilith. She had asked me not to call her Lily, even though I wanted to. She didn't go by anything else. I still liked the name. Truthfully, it reminded me of a video game character, a happy thought for me, but also of Fraiser.

As I crossed the street to get to the restaurant, I saw her. I wasn't completely sure it was her. She was across the street putting money in the parking meter. She wasn't looking my way. I kept walking, past the restaurant, and down the street where I looked across to a Spanish restaurant to see who was bartending. Didn't matter. I turned around and started back for the Italian restaurant. I wanted to make a joke about her jay-walking. No. That wouldn't be a very good start. She noticed me when she was halfway across the street. Then she was creamed by a Rolls Royce. I'm just kidding. She made it across just fine. We greeted each other and I went in for a hug. She was very pretty. She had orange hair similar to the normal light red of a natural redhead. It had been dyed this beautiful color for Halloween. She had gone as the mad hatter. She was wearing jeans and a tank top, underneath a short-cut leather jacket. High heels. I had told her to wear jeans instead of a dress. I didn't really like dresses. Too one-dimensional. Not as much in common with my outfits.

We had been talking to each other already and I was comfortable with her, though we hadn't met in person. At least not in this life, it seemed.

I held the door open then followed her in. "Reservation for Michael," I said.

"We only have space open in this room," said the hostess, pointing to the room that I had requested in the reservation. Had she read the notes? I doubted it, but it somehow worked out the way I wanted it to. A date was better in this room, where it was quieter. The other room was more casual, and always busy. We sat down at the table. I ordered two glasses of prosecco for us to start. It was easy for us to talk to each other. We had a lot in common. We both liked the same movies. She was an aficionado of cult movies. I had studied video production. We talked about her past. I didn't like to talk about myself. I talked about what I did now, working at restaurants and writing books. I didn't mention the parts that would make me look crazy. She told me about how important religion was to her. She was Christian. I told her that I was Catholic, which was technically true. I was raised Catholic and it was the only organized religion I had ever been involved in. I was more into Buddhism at this point, but believed that all religions were right, as long as it was about practicing love and tolerance, not judgment. She told me that God was a very important part of her life and continued on in that vein for a while. I ate a lot faster than she did, but she was the one doing most of the talking.

She continued to talk about her family, and how everyone in her life was fake and judgmental. Part of me worried that she might be projecting. The reality was living in a toxic household. They were in their own world, which was looking out at her in a negative way most of the time. That didn't seem fair to me. People lacked awareness. Not her, the people in her past, and even her close family, it seemed. She asked me why I liked her, because she thought that she was weird. I always thought I was too. I have just been better at hiding it lately. In a better niche for my type. The meal went well. We almost walked out without paying, by accident. Nice one.

We moved on to a beer house nearby, and talked more over a pumpkin ale. After that we went to my apartment with some excuse other than what would probably happen. It wasn't so silly as, "you have to see my fish tank," but it accomplished the same goal. I opened the prosecco. She noticed the chocolates, and I told her that I had gotten it for her. She looked through the things that were readily available around the room, while I put on music. We sat on the couch together and continued to talk. She sat on the right of me. I always sat in the middle. No one else had ever done that. They always sat on the other side. I knew she was different. We kissed. She took my shirt off. I took hers off. It was escalating. I had to stop. She needed to know the truth before we continued. I owed it to her. Especially when religion was so important to her.

"Lilith, there is something you need to know before we continue," I said.

"I knew it, you're married aren't you?" She asked.

"No."

"Gay?"

"Ha ha, no."

"My friends asked me if you were gay when they saw your pictures."

"What? No, I'm not gay."

"Then what is it?"

"I'm a demon."

"What?

"I'm a demon."

"A demon?"

"Yeah, you know, like bad, I guess. There is something inside of me that comes out sometimes. It is not really a choice. I was born this way."

"I know."

"You know? What do you mean?"

"I have a confession to make too," she said. "I already knew about you before we met."

"You did? Then why did you agree to see me?"

"It doesn't bother me. I think it's really cool, actually. I respect it."

"You like it? Have you been watching me?"

"Yes. Well, not me, at first. There is a group of us. We look for people like you and invite them to teach us about them."

"Demons? You invite them into your life?"

"Yes. We are fascinated by them. It was one of the reasons I wanted to meet you."

"Oh. Then do you really like me, or is it just because I am a demon?"

"I do like you. We have so much in common, and it really does feel like we have known each other for a lot longer than we have."

"Maybe it was in a past life."

"Maybe it was." I was surprised she agreed, because of her religious beliefs. Obviously there was more too her than I knew. Including spying on me.

"It's okay, you don't have to worry," said Lilith. "We are your friends, not your enemies. Especially me. I really like you, and want to spend as much time with you as I can."

"You have to know, it's just a small part of me. I'm just a normal person most of the time. I never do demon things by choice. It's always out of necessity, and something that I can't control."

"You don't have to defend yourself to me. I accept you for who you are. For what you are." She kissed me. The conversation was over. The touching escalated. I can't talk about the rest. Soon we were picking up our clothes from around the room, off the floor, and putting them on.

"Will you turn me into a demon?" she asked. Was that what this had been about? How would I ever know if she really liked me for who I was? Were those empty kisses? They didn't feel empty. It's easy to persuade men. Would she have asked me before if that was the case? I had already gotten what I wanted. If that is what this was about. It wasn't for me. I wanted to get to know her. To spend more time with her. I really liked her.

"I don't think it works like that," I said. "I'm not a vampire or anything. It is something you are or aren't, as far as I can tell."

"Oh," she said, sounding disappointed. "I just always wanted to be immortal, like you. To not have to worry about being weak."

"I don't think I am immortal. Honestly, there aren't a lot of advantages to it. If anything, I feel more persecuted than ever. There are groups of people I don't even know about, both loving and hating me, never having even met me. I just found out I was a demon, and it seems like I was the last one clued in on it. I wouldn't wish this on anyone."

"Don't say that. You are special. You were here before us. It's a blessing."

"I think you should go," I said.

"Can I see you again?"

"I don't know. I guess so, but only because there are unanswered questions I have for you."

"Okay," she said, giving me a kiss on the cheek, then heading out. What had I gotten myself into this time?

Chapter 24
Immortality

I had a lot of questions for Zach, as usual. He would be the one who could give me answers. I invited him to my apartment, so we could talk in private, uninterrupted. I was starting to gather that there was only so much we should say out loud at work. I made a pot of coffee and we sat down on the couch to talk.

"What's on your mind?" Zach asked me.

"All kinds of things. As if it couldn't get any more complicated than it already was."

"Ha, oh yeah?"

"Yeah. So I met this girl..."

"Another girl? What happened with you and Ella? Didn't I see you two leave together the other day?"

"That's not important. We spent a night together, but I don't think it will happen again."

"She seems like a really nice girl."

"Demon-girl."

"We just say girl," Zach said, referring to the demon community.

"Anyway, I met this other girl. She is human. A regular girl, but she doesn't want to be."

"Ah. That's too bad. For her I mean. She should be happy with who she is."

"I know. That's what I told her. I was happy when I thought I was human. That's not all, she belongs to this group that tracks demons."

"There is a group that follows us?"

"Yeah. Some kind of worshippers or something."

"Are any of them hunters?"

"Not that I know of," I said. "She is the only one I have met so far, and it seems that they just want to know more about us."

"Ah, and what is your plan for that?"

"What do you mean?"

"I mean, what are you going to do?"

"Well, I thought I would meet with them since they seem to already know about me."

"Do you trust them?"

"I trust the girl I know, but I do feel like she is hiding something from me."

"It could be dangerous. Send me the details and I will stop by to make sure everything is okay."

"I will. It would be nice if I wasn't the only demon there. I mean, you have so much more experience and everything. I do have a few questions too, though."

"Go ahead. I am here for you, buddy."

"Are we immortal?"

"That's a complicated question. There are many facets to immortality. Every living thing has a life essence. That essence is carried on from life to life, reincarnated, so to speak. Demons are included. The only difference is that most demons want to be demons. They do bad things so that they have no chance of incarnating as anything but a demon. The energy, like any other, can come back in a variety of ways, based on what we do while we are here on earth. We believe that by being good in this life, there is a chance for us to come back as a cleaner life form. If angels can fall from heaven, why can't demons rise up to it? So, in the way that most beings can all come back in a new incarnation, everyone is immortal to an end. The only exception is vampires and other beings that surrender their energy to be kept on earth. When those beings die, there is no continuance. It is a final ending. So, while we may not be on earth in this form for very long, we will come back in some way or another. This also helps prevent metal and physical decay that occurs from cell regeneration. Mutation and other irregularities. Cells regenerate, and over time they mutate causing defects. The biggest problem they face, is that with time, comes decay. It is a natural part of existence. If any of these cancers grew in an immortal being, there would be nothing to keep them sane, so dying is a way to bring their energy to a new body. Some demons are able to keep their memories, others aren't. We come back with superhuman powers to make it easier for us to reach our ends. You already know that we can be wounded, even killed with specialty weapons, in that way we are mortal. You in particular. As long as you are wearing your cross, you are in control, but you are also vulnerable. You are just as vulnerable as any other human, as long as you are under its influence. If you get mortally wounded while wearing it, you will die. Your lifespan will be that of a normal person. If you take it off, you will be able to heal, but you will also have less control over yourself. It's better this way. Don't see yourself as different from anyone else. That's what the group is all about. It's one of the steps to surviving a normal life and moving on responsibly."

"Wow. How do you know so much?"

"Inherently, demons do have a much longer life span than humans. I am not nearly as young as I look. I have been studying with different groups and organizations for a long time. It has also afforded me control over myself. I don't need the restraint that your cross offers, and I am not interested in a normal life. I know this distances me from most of society, but it also allows me to help friends, like you."

"Oh. The help you have given me is much appreciated. I don't know what I would do without you."

"Thanks, buddy. I feel the same way about you. I mean, I haven't had a lot of close friends, outside of my immediate family that I could be honest with in the past hundred years. Not many demons were given the choice that you were. They concede to their nature because that is all they ever knew. Like psychopaths that aren't used as soldiers."

We enjoyed the coffee and continued to talk for a while longer. I wrote down the details of the demon lovers meeting that I was supposed to attend that night and gave them to Zach. I would be more comfortable having someone there to support me. I didn't really know what to expect from these people.

"I want you to have this," Zach said, handing me the messenger bag he had walked in with. "It is a hunting kit."

"Hunting? Demon-hunting?" I asked.

"Among other things. I hope you never have to use it, but you should have it in case something ever comes up and I am not around. Most of it is self-explanatory. There is a book in there for the rest."

"Thank you. I appreciate it, though I don't think I need it."

"Better safe than sorry."

Zach left, and I spend the rest of the day preparing for the meeting that night.

I got a text from Lilith. "Sorry, I won't be able to make it to the meeting with you tonight! I hope it goes really well, they are expecting you."

"What? Why not?" I texted back.

"We have a lead on another being. Will fill you in tomorrow."

Well that sucked. I didn't really even want to go to the meeting, yet alone without Lilith. Maybe I should just stay home. But they are expecting me, and they know where I live. I was obligated to go.

Chapter 25
The Society

At eight o'clock that night, I knocked on the steel door to what looked like an abandoned building. A slat in the door opened to reveal two eyes glaring at me from inside.

"Name?" Came a voice on the other side of the door.

"Michael," I replied.

"Guest or speaker?"

"Guest speaker?"

"Who invited you?"

"Lilith."

The slat shut and there was silence all around. I heard bolts sliding, then the door opened and I was invited in much more enthusiastically than I had been greeted. There was an angry looking big guy, who must have been a bouncer and the guy who had spoken through the door. There was now a much friendlier person there along with him, as well as a girl by his side. He was taller than me, at least six foot two, had dark hair and a neatly trimmed beard. He was wearing big round sunglasses that reflected most of what he looked at. He had a smile that I wouldn't be able to forget, like he was in charge of the universe. I wondered if he was on something.

"Greetings," he said, "I am Harry." He pulled me in for a hug, which was awkward because I didn't know him at all.

"Michael," I said back, after he had let me go.

"I see Lilith has a sense of humor," he said, looking at me. "But I'll wait for the presentation before I judge. You came on a good night. There is a full moon. Everyone is here tonight. You are the guest of honor."

"Uh, thank you," I said.

"Come on in, get yourself a drink, what do you like? Beer, wine... blood?"

"What? No, wine is fine. Red wine. French if you have it."

"Ha ha ha! Get this man some wine!" Harry yelled. Someone behind him took off to go find some. "Anyway, I'm the one in charge here. I'll be up there with you on stage when this whole thing begins. See if you can mingle a little bit before we get started. I think they'll get a kick out of you."

I didn't do a lot of mingling. I sipped on the wine that the guy in the background had scrounged up and brought me. It was decent, but not French. Was he serious about the blood? It was one of the strangest groups of people I had ever seen. The demon lovers. Half of them were wearing beyond belief outfits that made them look like something out of a steampunk convention, and the rest just looked like normal people. The lighting was bad, and most of the people were standing around the bar or dance floor. There were ten rows of chairs setup in front of a stage. I imagined that is where the presentation would be.

A girl with half of her head shaved came up to me and started talking. For some reason I found her attractive, though she would not be so conventionally. The skin that was exposed, beside her face, was covered in tattoos. She had piercings in places I didn't know possible. And huge eyes that accentuated her small round skull.

"This your first time?" she asked. "It's okay. We're all really cool here. You don't have to worry."

"Yeah, it is." I replied, not knowing what else to say.

"I'm Brittney," she said.

"Brittney?" I asked, surprised.

"Yeah, what, I don't look like a Brittney?"

"No, you don't."

"Looks can be deceiving, but what's in a name anyway?"

"I'm Michael."

"Oh. You do look like an Michael. I guess that makes one of us." We were interrupted when a muscular guy who was wearing biker clothes bumped into me and spilled my glass of wine.

"Hey, watch where you're going!" the guy said, looking like he was about to take a swing at me. A cute girl, about my height, with blonde hair, quickly stepped in and grabbed him by the arm.

"Stop it Frank, don't you know who that is?" She said to him.

"What? Who?" Frank asked her.

"He's the *you know what*." Frank's eyes noticeably widened and I could see that he was suddenly afraid, not just by his change in tone.

"Ohh. I'm sorry," Frank said to me. "It was an honest mistake." He nodded his head and slowly backed away, with his palms held up facing me.

"It's you?" Brittney asked, with a laugh. "That is too good. I can't wait to see this. Why didn't you tell me? You've caused quite the stir."

"I don't know what you're talking about," I said.

"I think you do, but I'll let you get away with it this time." She kept eyeing me up and down as she walked away to get another drink.

"There you are," came a male voice from behind me. "We need you on stage." It was an AV guy with a headset. He led me to where I was supposed to be sitting, right on stage next to a podium with a few more chairs next to me. There were other people sitting in them as well. The lights went up and down a few times to signal everyone to be seated. The crowd took their places. I could see everyone briefly. Brittney, Frank, the girl with the blonde hair, oh, and Zach, sitting nonchalantly near the back. There were two other guys I recognized sitting in the audience. The thugs from the alley. Demon hunters. Great. I wonder if Zach noticed them too. This meeting had been compromised. Even with the big angry guy at the door. Was he even alive still? Stop it, he's probably fine. All you needed to do to get in, was lie. I doubt most of the demon lovers had ever seen each other in person. It was probably more of an online forum or something that just spread rumors. It was stupid for me to come here. They weren't ready for this. The lights went down and it stayed dark for a moment. There was a spotlight on the podium and Harry walked up.

"Greetings!" he said, addressing the crowd. "A big welcome, and thank you to all of the lovers who could be here with us tonight, as well as our special guest, Michael." He waved his hand toward me, and there was applause. "Many of you know our star finder, Lilith, and as always, she is too busy searching to be here with us tonight. Her workgroup has put together a presentation for us, as well as a special surprise at the end. I think all of you want to know why Michael is so special. All in good time." There was a noticeable, "aww" from the audience, as Harry continued to speak on about other things. "First off, all recording and monitoring of any sort here tonight, is strictly forbidden unless it has been otherwise approved by a moderator. We need our guests to always feel comfortable, and their anonymity is our priority. Nothing ruins fun faster than a viral video that scares every creature from ever wanting to talk to us again. This has to be a safe place for everyone. Human or not. Now, this is one of the first nights, in quite a long time that we have had such a special guest, and I won't waste any more time talking about it, instead of letting the experts do their thing."

The people in the three chairs next to me got up to speak together. One was a nerdy looking guy, skinny, couldn't be more than twenty. The leader was more handsome, but still had acne. He was clearly a little older and more experienced. Maybe he was his brother. They looked somewhat alike. The third was a girl with curly dark hair past her shoulders. She was average looking and not very memorable. Probably perfect for spying on creatures they thought might not be human. Beyond human, as they called it. Nobody in the demon world kept score, we were all just different, not better or worse. Their names were Ben, Jake, and Amanda. I found that out when a projector started up and showed a slide with their photographs, names under them, and the title of their presentation, "Demon's Among Us." They certainly had a flair for the dramatic.

The next slide had a picture of me. Ben, the older one, started talking. "This is Michael," he said. "Looks like an ordinary man, doesn't he? Well, there is much more than meets the eye. Something deeper, and darker, inside of this innocent looking person." I felt a little like I was being put on trial, but figured that they were young and wanted to make an impact with their presentation more than judge me. The next slide showed the alley next to Louie's with police tape. "This is the first noted incident. It was what flagged us to the possibility of demons being this close to us. As you will see from the video footage we took from the courthouse across the street, things are not quite normal about what happened the night before." Thank you to our anonymous detective on duty who donated this footage, and kept it from the police. The next slide had a video on it. He clicked his pointer but nothing happened. It went too far ahead in the slides to a bank. Then back to the video slide. He tried again, but it wouldn't work. Someone came up and minimized the presentation, then clicked the video, full-screen, and it worked this time. "Sorry about that," he said. The video was of the alley, the night before. Nothing out of the ordinary was happening. Someone was smoking a cigarette in the alley. Then I saw myself walk by and stop. My hands became claws. I watched in disbelief, as I slammed the man's head against the wall, then threw him down the alley. I went off-screen somewhere, and he started crawling away. His body was pulled under a car and a torrent of blood came flooding out. It had been me. That wasn't how I remembered it. That was how it happened when Jenny did these things... in my head. I was the one doing it. The entire audience was silent, as the video came to an end. I was mortified. Suddenly a single clap was heard. Someone was clapping, then everyone joined in. They all stood up, cheering, roaring, except for Zach and the demon hunters. Zach had his hand over his face, like he didn't want to see what was happening. If it had been my fault, it had also been his fault.

"Thank you," Ben said, "Thank you, but there is much more to come." He clicked to the next slide, showing the bank. I knew that bank. It was my bank. Until the branch shut it down after the massacre. "Guadalupe Bank, hardly after the first incident, there is a massacre of over a dozen people. The police have nothing to go on, but this video footage of a victim escaping." The video showed me crawling out of the bank, and stumbling to run away. "He was there," Ben said, pointing to me. The only witness to what happened, the police not even knowing that he was the cause. There were ooo's coming from the audience. Impressed by what I had done. It hadn't been my choice. They really liked this kind of thing?

"Here is video footage of Michael walking to work two days later with no visible wounds whatsoever." The presentation continued on like this. It showed me catch the bullet, barley missing Zach on the screen. They were so close to knowing his secret. Then what they showed next surprised me. It was a black SUV in a parking lot in the middle of the night.

"As you may know, one of our teams was tracking another demon," said Ben. "We followed him here, where we believed he was going to take his next victim, but we were pleasantly surprised by the turn of events that unfolds." The amateur footage showed me walking up to the car and getting thrown back. We know the rest. I shot the demon in the head as the girl ran away. Furious applause from the audience. They had never witnessed a demon-slaying. My reputation was solidified with them. I was this big scary demon that they could worship. The presentation was coming to an end. The lights came up and Ben finished his speech. "And so, here before you today we have this very special, honored guest, Michael. A demon among us. Though we need no further convincing, there is a special surprise for you tonight. We get to watch him feed, right before our very eyes." The audience gasped in surprised pleasure. Two assistants rolled a chair onto the stage, in the chair was a figure, covered by a sheet. They weren't going to let me speak, were they?

You could cut the tension with a knife. Everyone was on the edge of their seats, waiting to see what was under the sheet. Harry walked onto the stage and over to the figure in the chair and pulled off the sheet. There was a girl tied to the chair. She had a sack over her head. Harry walked to the microphone to make a short speech. "The moment we have all been waiting for. For years we have been in this dedicated organization, looking for things beyond us, and tonight, we have found it. Michael will be our honored guest every week from now on. We will feed him all he likes, in hopes that he will share his secrets with us. Now Michael, if you would come up here and show us who you really are." They wanted me to kill the girl. They wanted to see me rip her apart. I wasn't planning on killing anyone. I am a good person. I stood up and walked over to Harry and the microphone.

"Hi," I said to the microphone, "Yes, I am Michael, and all of what you saw was true. I did hurt those people. I am a demon, but that's not someone I want to be. I am a good person. I have tried, as long as I have known, just to live a normal life, and have fought to keep that part of me from taking over."

"Now now," said Harry. "No need to be modest. We know it's in your nature. Maybe you just have to see what she looks like, sitting there helpless. We can untie her if you like, and give you a chance to chase her." He pulled the sack off of the girls head. Sitting there, tied to the chair, was the unmistakable face of the girl from the demon attack. I remembered her in the black SUV, scared out of her mind, when I confronted the demon I ended up shooting. No. I had saved her from him, why would I want to hurt her?

"She is the only witness to what happened that night, I'm sure you wouldn't mind tying up the loose ends," Harry said. All eyes were on me.

"Look, I'm sorry. I came here to talk, not to hurt anyone. I don't know what kind of things you are into, but I never hurt people by choice," I said. The crowd was growing restless. People started booing, and throwing things at me. Maybe they wanted to incite me to violence, hoping I would turn. I heard Frank yell, "Coward!" from somewhere in the audience. Zach was about to stand up, but instead, the demon hunters did. The two thugs that I thought were trying to mug me that night on my way home. They both pulled out guns and pointed them around the room at everyone.

"Nobody move!" said one of the demon hunters. "I am Gabriel Luis Miller. I am a demon hunter, and that is my sister!" He was pointing to the girl who was tied up. The crowd gasped. The shorter demon hunter stayed behind in the crowd, as Gabriel walked up on to the stage. "My father was a professional demon hunter. He taught us everything he knew, but nothing could have prepared us for something like this. We got in over our heads when my sister tried to challenge that demon you saw in the video. We know that Michael is a demon, but we have seen that he is a good person. He saved my sister, and for that I will always be grateful. The real monsters are right here in front of me today. All of you in the crowd, encouraging this sort of thing. You people should be ashamed of yourselves, wanting demons to inflict pain on the world. Now, you will let my sister go, and we will end this nonsense once and for all."

"Alright," said Harry, holding his hands up for everyone to stay calm. "It's okay. I understand where you are coming from. We know when we are beat." He looked at me with an angry stare, wishing I would rip them all apart. He walked over to the girl and got behind her to undo the ropes. "But what kind of a show would this be without a little blood?" he asked. They didn't know that Harry had a knife. He pulled it across the girls throat, spilling her blood all over the front of her shirt and threw his head up laughing like he had completely lost his mind.

"No!" yelled Gabriel. Harry held up the knife and started to run toward Gabriel, but Gabriel lifted his gun first, shooting Harry through the forehead before he was attacked. The body fell to the ground and slid another six inches toward Gabriel. Harry wasn't getting back up. Behind his body, the girl tied to the chair was still bleeding all over her white dress. Gabriel ran over to her trying to put the blood back in, but there was no way it could work. He looked around frantically. "Help me, someone help me. You have to save her." At first, the audience was silent, and only his pathetic cries could be heard as Gabriel tried to cling to his sister's life. He looked at everyone, including me, knowing that there was nothing we could do. The audience erupted into panic, and attacked the other demon hunter, beating him to death, then they turned on Gabriel. He was screaming as they grabbed him and dragged him down into the audience. Then a piercing roar made everything stand still. They looked to the back of the crowd, where a seven foot figure was standing with red eyes, and long sharp claws for fingers. The whole crowd got on their knees and worshipped him. It was Zach, in demon form.

"Michael," he called, in a deep scratchy voice. "This is why people must not know about us. There are rules for a reason. Take off your cross." I hesitated. "Take it off!" He roared at me. This wasn't going to be pretty. I took off my cross and put it in my pocket. Immediately, I was filled with heat, fire rushing in. Demon Zach looked at me and spoke, "ipsum daemonium revelare." I felt my fingers extending into sharper than steel claws. My teeth found their way into pointed fangs for tearing up meat. My vision turned red. No Jenny this time. Just me. This time I would have to watch myself kill them. Zach started ripping people apart, left and right. I still didn't want to kill them. There was a gasp of awe, as they stared at my demon form. One of them ran up to me to attack, and I swung my arm at him, throwing him twenty feet across the room into the wall. I was still conscious. The darkness in me was not taking over. There was screaming and disgusting crunches as Zach ripped people apart with his teeth. It was nothing like in the movies. There was no soundtrack to lighten things up, just sounds of death. People were slipping in blood as they tried to run away, but there was nowhere to go. The doors were locked. Pretty soon no one was left standing but the demon Zach, and me, up on stage, frozen. We both turned back to our human forms. He walked over to me and put his hand on my shoulder.

"This is the only way it could be," he said to me. "Now, get the laptop so we can destroy the hard drive. No one needs to know about us. It never leads to anything good. I retrieved the keys from the dead bouncer, and grabbed the laptop, trying to leave the building without stepping on any body parts. This did not go well. Lilith was not going to be happy. I had to see her before she found out. Zach went behind the bar and found the house phone. He dialed a number then held the phone to his ear.

"Three, six, nine, three," he said into the receiver. "We need a cleanup crew at this location. Yes. Demon hunters, and worshippers. Not good people. We had to act under article thirteen. No, there was no other choice, I will have a full report by Friday." He left the receiver off the hook and walked out to the parking lot.

"Let's go," he said to me. We both got in his truck.

"How did you get in? Did you tell them you were a guest?"

"No, I told them I was a spectator, and mentioned Lilith."

"I'm glad you were there," I said to him. "I don't know what I would have done."

"It's okay. I know. There was nothing you could do. There are bad people out there, just as well as bad demons. You can't judge either one outside of the moment.

I'm going to drop you off downtown so you can walk from there. It would be good if someone saw you in this area. Stop by a bar and have a drink so that you have an alibi."

My mind was whirling. I needed a drink. Zach dropped me off downtown, after giving me a knowing nod. I nodded back. We could never speak of this. I walked up San Francisco Street and stopped by the new dive bar that was on the left side. All of the bars were centrally located, right next to each other, except for the one at the rail station. There were birds decorating this one. A weird place, with weird people, it even had birds on a TV screen, but I was in luck. Someone I knew was there. I said hi to him and had a brief conversation before excusing myself to get a drink at the bar. I got a pumpkin ale and ended up playing a few games of pool with different people. That would be really good for an alibi. My mind wasn't in it, of course. Finally, we lost and decided to go our separate ways for the night. I hoped my friend would be sober enough the next day to remember this. He was a guy I worked with at Louie's. He had a driver picking him up in a few minutes, and I told him I would be walking home.

I only had a few drinks, and was still riding on an adrenaline high. The events of the day were running through my mind as I crossed through the plaza, up Washington Street. A lot of the streets were named after presidents. I made the mistake of walking by Louie's, and looking down the alley as I went.

Not surprisingly, there was Jenny in the alley biting someone's neck. Not like she did with me, closer to the front where the artery is this time. Not the kind of thing I wanted to deal with right now. I thought I was going to be done with these hallucinations. I looked just long enough to make eye contact with her and the other girl she was with, and kept walking. Great. Even worse. It was Lilith. Now I could get blamed for that one too. As I got to the stoplight, I made sure that I had put my cross back on from earlier. I had. It was resting safely on my chest. I looked over my shoulder as I walked back to my apartment, expecting to be chased by my own mind. I even looked in the sky, maybe she was a bat. The red agate stones on my wrist started to glow. "Don't look at me like that," I told the bracelet. "You are the one who is supposed to make me more aware." I was looking forward to a good night's sleep now, more than ever.

Chapter 26

Understanding

It turns out the events of that day were yet to be over. Assuming dreams that night counted as part of the day. It was time for another dream-story from one of the previous owners of the bracelet. "I'm just never going to get any peace," I said to myself.

In this new place, that looked similar to the last visions, a man with a round face walked up to me. He was wearing what looked like a dress. It was a typical piece of clothing in this part of the world. He had the bracelet on as well, which was expected, but clued me in that this was not just a dream.

"Ah, welcome," said the man. "To my story. I am Ali, that was the name I went by in life. When I was young, I was always a very light hearted person." The background faded into Ali's story. I saw him as a child, laughing and playing with other children. I could see that everyone he was around would be smiling when they saw him come in the room. I watched him grow older into a very happy man. I didn't understand where this was going. Everyone so far had been suffering from the start. This man seemed to have no problems at all.

"I got married to Shandra, the most beautiful woman in the world," he said. "I didn't know life could be this glorious. Everything was perfect with us from the start. We loved each other so dearly. I worked hard to give her everything she could ever want and spent my every waking moment thinking about how I could make her happier. Then the answer came. We had a darling baby boy together." I saw Ali with Shandra and their baby. There was so much happiness in this place. It was more than ideal. I never imagined people could be so happy from such small things.

"Yes, everything was perfect," Ali said, nodding to me outside of the vision. "I loved my wife, and our son. Nothing in the world could be more dear to me. I was too happy with what I had to see the impermanence of life. When he was only four years old, my son was killed by a drunk driver. Where I am from it is not uncommon for people to be killed by cars. There is no accountability, or responsible driving. There was nothing that could be done about it. Shandra was inconsolable. We had lost the most precious thing in our lives, and there would be no getting it back. I suddenly found that I was not laughing or smiling anymore. I vowed revenge on whomever had done this to us. I would not be able to live another day without getting even. I went to a local shop and bought a gun. I followed the man for two days before I jumped out at him, gun in hand. I told him he had killed my son, and that there was no justice. He would have to die. He apologized and begged me for his life. He knew it had been a horrible accident and it had been plaguing his mind as well. He had not drank another drop of alcohol since it had happened. It did not matter to me. I shot him in the head while he was on his knees crying. I walked away, feeling like a part of me had died too. I was not a cruel or violent man. I had always been the happy one. Not today. I told my wife about what I had done. She said she understood, but did not want to be close to me after that. Our son had died. Nothing could bring him back or make it better. A month later my wife got very sick and she died in the hospital. I was there by her side the whole time, watching her life drain out. I vowed on that day that I would never smile again. This time I had no one to blame directly, so I accused the universe of conspiring against me. I blamed existence for not wanting beautiful things to thrive. For hating happiness, and leaving me here like this. I cursed everything, and all of life. There was no remorse, no solace. Just a big hole inside of me, where love had been."

I looked at Ali while he was telling the story and felt sorry for him. I had not experienced this kind of loss in my lifetime and don't know how I would deal with it when the time came.

"That is not all," he said. "There is more to my story." I hadn't even considered that there was no mention of the bracelet up to this point. "Having lost everything, I left my home to find answers. I vowed that I would not eat until I found what I was looking for. In my mind, I would win either way, whether I found the answers or simply starved to death and was able to join them. It was only a day later that someone stopped me. He said he was sorry for what I was going through, and promised me that if I wore the bracelet he gave me, I would find what I was looking for. I did not believe him, but I accepted out of politeness and put on the bracelet. I traveled from town to town asking the most wise of people why I was experiencing this. Most of them gave me the same answers, impermanence, and life is suffering. I already knew that much. I wanted to know why it was happening to me. So suddenly. It wasn't fair. I somehow managed to stay alive for two months, and I knew it was the bracelet giving me the energy to keep going. I should have been dead by then. I tried to pull off the bracelet, but it had attached itself to me. There was no way to get it off. I would have to suffer the rest of my life like this. That man had cursed me. I swore at him, wherever he was, whatever life he was ruining now, and I laid down in the grass next to a river. I stared up at the night sky sad that there was nothing I could do. I felt so helpless. I couldn't even die. So alone. So empty. Please, just give me answers, I begged the universe, tears in my eyes. Then I heard a voice in my head speak to me. It wasn't exactly inside of me though, it sounded like it was coming from everywhere at once. "Can't you see that it's all perfect?" I lost it. I cried harder and angrier than ever. How could that be my answer? Perfect? Perfect that my son and wife had died? Perfect that I had murdered a man who was begging for forgiveness? Perfect that I was miserable and alone? It was just rubbing salt in the wound. I screamed into the empty landscape. I screamed my lungs out and sobbed until it hurt. I cried for so long and so hard that I couldn't feel the pain anymore. Then came release. I let go. I was so overwhelmed that there was nothing left to feel. I surrendered to all of it. Then I realized that I had been looking at it all wrong. None of it had been malicious. These things had been accidents. No one made them happen. It was just part of how things were, but I was taking it personally. I didn't understand until now that there was no one to blame. It is just the way things were. On top of that, I was doing no justice to their memory. I should have been honoring their existence and the good times we had together. By being this other person I was betraying who I was meant to be. Who I was deep down inside. A good person. A happy person. One who would make others smile just by walking in the room. So I went to the nearest market and was given food. Everyone assumed I was a beggar, because of the way I looked, yet they had wonder in their eyes when they looked at me. They could tell there was something different about me. That I was finally free. Free to be what I was meant to be. I vowed that I would only make the best of life from then on. That I would look on everything with understanding instead of judgment. That is what I wish for you as well." Ali put his hand on my shoulder and bowed his head. My problems looked so small in comparison. Then I woke up, back to the real world.

Chapter 27
Not What I Expected

I understood now. None of it was my fault. Everybody was making choices around me that were leading them to all of the things that were happening. I know that whatever was inside of me killed those people at the bank, and in the alley, without my consciousness. I didn't make it happen or have a say in the matter. That didn't seem fair, but these are the cards I was dealt. There was nothing I could do but fight it my whole life. Understanding was half the battle. Now that I knew, and was aware, it should be under my control. I wouldn't allow things to happen that I didn't want. There was always one last choice to make.

I was working at Louie's that night. It was a nice break from my current norm. It was fun seeing all of the people who work there. I only work there two days a week, and the ones who work on the same day as I do are usually the same. The older crew I don't see as often, but they were there this night. We talked about their vacations, plans to find other jobs, and all of the general life problems that servers talk about. It was actually relaxing. I got hugs from most of them. Then Jenny came in to bartend, and kept giving me strange looks. Maybe it was because she heard about my date earlier that week. I knew she liked me, but it was too late for any of that now. I was finally over it. Over Jenny. She could have her own life and I would have mine. Working together twice a week was fine, but that's all it was now. I didn't even think about her anymore. At least, that's what I thought until the other night. I don't know how it happened that my mind created that, especially after having the chance for carnage at the demon lovers meeting.

"Hey," she said to me. "We need to talk."

"I don't think we do, actually," I said back to her. "I'd like to keep this less personal, if you don't mind."

"It's just... about what you saw last night."

"I didn't see anything, and frankly I don't care what you were doing. It's none of my business and I don't need any more complication in my life. Whatever you were doing, by all means, knock yourself out." Wait. Was this all in my head? Was she talking about something else? Maybe she saw me at the bar earlier. No, just stop. It doesn't matter what she is talking about. She is not playing a role in your life anymore. "Honestly, I just don't care at all."

"Oh," she said. She picked up a glass to polish as I walked away back to my side work. I wasn't going to get involved with any more drama, whether it was real or in my head. I smiled, thinking about how that went. It worked for me. I stood up for myself. The night went well. Jenny and I had casual conversation during the night, but it wasn't brought up again. Finally, when the night was over, and the paperwork done, I had a glass of wine before heading home.

When I got to my apartment and turned on my cellphone, I received all the texts that people had sent throughout the day. Nothing special, but one stood out. Lilith had texted me the dreaded phrase, "We need to talk." Good thing I wasn't in a relationship with her, or that could be bad. Oh, wait, all her friends are dead and it's partially my fault. Maybe I should be worried. I do owe her an explanation, and she is a loose end. What am

I saying? I texted her back, "Come on over." Forty minutes later, I saw her walking by the picture window, and I opened the door for her.

"You have to invite me in," she said. It was starting already. Part of me feared this might happen. I hoped it was in my head. That it hadn't been real.

"Please come in," I said, gesturing with my right arm for her to walk past me into the apartment.

"Did you drive here?" I asked.

"No. I walked, why do you ask?" she said.

"No reason. Would you like a glass of wine?"

"I don't like wine anymore," she said. "Michael?" she said as if asking me a question.

"Yeah," I said from the kitchen, as I opened a bottle of Bordeaux and poured myself a glass.

"All of my friends are dead."

"Ah. I thought you might say that." Awkward. "They wanted me to kill this girl they had tied to a chair, and there were demon hunters that started attacking, and before you knew it, BAM, everyone was dead."

"It's okay. I understand," she said.

"What?"

"I said it's okay. I have new friends now. I never really felt that close to them, that's why I was never at the meetings. It sounds like it was a good thing that I wasn't there. Would you have killed me too?"

"I don't know. It all happened so fast. I didn't plan on anything like that happening. There were no survivors."

"It's okay. I understand. That's why I love you so much. You and I were meant to be together. We can be immortals together, forever."

"Lilith, I told you, I'm not immortal, I'm a demon."

"But you can be, just one bite. I can do it for you."

"We don't even know if that works on demons. On top of that, this isn't something I chose. I never wanted to be a demon, I just wanted to be me and this darkness inside of me kept coming up and doing things without my permission."

"Please? It will only take a second. It will make you better. Stronger. More intuitive. It breaks down all of the barriers and levels of reality. You are going to love it. Maybe what is inside of you is the real you."

"I can't. Why did you do this to yourself? You were perfect the way you were."

"You didn't even know me! It was only one night. You have no idea what it's like to suffer the way I have, knowing that everyone around you is going to die, including yourself. I could have saved them if I had met Jenny sooner."

"You are glorifying this. How much fun is it going to be to have to eat people to survive? Are you that disconnected from the world? You are going to have to hurt a lot of people."

"They deserve it. I had to go through hell, and so do they. Life isn't all glorious, and being human sucks! I am finally something greater, and you are trying to make me feel bad about it."

"I just don't understand why you would make a choice like that."

"You would if you were human your whole life," she retorted.

"As far as I knew, I was."

"Well, I can't go back now, and this is so much better. I thought you would be happy for me. I am stronger, faster, and more beautiful than I ever could have imagined possible. Everything I had to worry about has fallen away. I can see so much more. So much further. Everything is brighter. Do you know what it's like to see clearly during the night? It's beautiful. Something I never could have experienced as a human. The world is so much more glorious. I wouldn't trade this for anything. I just want you to join me, please, it will only take a second. You will thank me for it. I know it."

"No one deserves to live forever," I said.

She forced herself on me, throwing her fangs toward my neck. It reminded me of Jenny. She had the same red eyes. Beautiful, glistening white teeth extending from her mouth. I surrendered, let in the darkness. It is time. I held my neck up for her. As soon as she got close to me she jumped back with a hiss, as if something had burned her. It woke me up, took me away from her charm.

"Agh," was the noise she made in despair, as she jumped back against the wine fridge. In the process she had flipped over the coffee table spilling the contents of the demon hunting kit Zach had left. "What is that?" she demanded.

I pulled out my cross, and let it fall against the outside of my shirt.

"Protection," I said. "It is meant to keep other people safe from me, but it appears it is keeping me safe from you."

"Get rid of it!" she yelled.

"I really thought things were going well between us. I think I was even growing to love you, though it has been such a short amount of time. Did you know that vampires are the only ones who really die when they are killed? I am so sorry that it had to happen this way."

"What do you mean?" she asked. I put my hand out, and the wooden stake that had fallen from the demon hunting kit was immediately attracted to it.

"I can't let you hurt anyone else. I feel like part of this is my fault," I said, moving closer to her. She held out her hands to shield herself from me and hissed as she was backed into the corner next to the wine fridge. "I feel really bad about this," I said. She looked up at me with sadness in her eyes. She had let me down. All she had wanted was for us to be happy together for the rest of eternity. Even though we hardly knew each other. I think she thought that being one of these beings created a kinship. Was it the last idea of a hopeless romantic? A love addict? Eternity was too much for me. Especially with someone who needs to kill others to survive. I gently brushed her hair back and kissed her on the forehead then shoved the stake into her chest, piercing her heart. The air was filled with dust as her whole body evaporated into nothingness. I wondered if I had made the right choice. Was it ever a choice? Zach had told me that sometimes there is only one way for things to go, and it has been pre-ordained. Good and bad. I couldn't tell which this one was.

Chapter 28
Moving Forward

The next day at work I told Zach about what happened.

"So Jenny really is a vampire?" he asked.

"It seems that way," I said.

"Then we have to take care of her."

"No. She is off limits. Leave her alone."

"Michael, she is a blood sucking creature of the night. She has to feed on people to survive. It would be irresponsible for us to let her live."

"Stop it. I said she's off limits and you need to listen to me. That is the final word. Let her have her life and we will have ours. There is no reason we can't coexist. Pretend I never told you."

"Boy, she really got to you, didn't she?"

"She is in my blood, even though I know we have no future together. I relish the thought of seeing her again, but I am the one who interrupted her life, not the other way around. We need to respect that and give her space."

"Alright. Just this once, but you have to know she will sell you out any chance she gets if it comes down to it."

"No, she won't. She doesn't know anything about me or us. She thinks I am a normal human being."

"What about all the stuff you told me?"

"I was wrong. You saw the video footage of me attacking those people. Jenny was never involved."

"But you didn't hesitate to destroy Lilith for the rest of eternity?"

"I had to. She was irresponsible. Doing it for the wrong reasons. Going down that path was her choice. We don't know anything about Jenny and her decisions. I think it's best if we forget this whole thing ever happened."

"You have someone looking out for you, the way all of this seems to get swept under the rug, but there is something I haven't been telling you. The Association wants to meet with you. I don't know what they want. It's not usually a good thing if they ask you to come to them. They heard about most of what happened, though none of it can be proven now that the evidence has been destroyed. They are the ones who sent the crew to investigate you, not knowing that they would go rouge and try to kill you. They have the final say in all demon affairs. If you agree to come with me and see them, I will never mention that Jenny is more than human. Is that fair?"

"Yes. More than fair. I agree."

"We can both go when we are off on Tuesday. There is a portal in the old native ruins a few hours outside of town. Be ready for me to pick you up at ten in the morning."

"Okay," I said. It was hard keeping our conversation light and friendly after that. Things were going to be awkward between us for a while it seemed. At least until all of this was straightened out.

The next day, I was working my other job at Louie's. It was the same shifts every week, and the same employees. That meant Jenny was bartending. We engaged in small talk as usual and I ended up mentioning the trip I would have to make.

"I am going on a day trip on Tuesday to the ancient ruins a few hours away."

"Is that where the petroglyphs are?" she asked.

"Yes, I think so."

"That sounds really fun, I should take my children there some time. I bet they would enjoy it, and they need the outdoor time."

"I'm hoping to be coming back that night, but would you do something for me?"

"Like what?" she asked, hesitantly. She was thinking of all the bad things I could ask for, her thought process driven by fear.

"I need someone to feed my cat, Ezekiel. It really shouldn't be for long, but I need to know that someone is there to check on him."

"I guess I could, you do live pretty close," she said.

"Thank you so much, you are a life saver. There is a key under the mat, he gets half a cup of dry food a day, all at once. He will eat it at his leisure."

"Would you mind if I brought my kids to see him? They love cats and we could never get one."

"That should be fine, but he may just run away and hide. He is a little bit of a scaredy-cat, he was a rescue."

"I understand."

Well that takes care of it. I have backup plans. Someone to watch over my life. I didn't know if the way Zach spoke of the Association was accurate or not, but shouldn't take any chances. I would go with my cross and bracelet, to protect myself. I really didn't know what to expect, but it was best to plan for the worst. After all, I had done really bad things, even if I wasn't doing them by choice.

Chapter 29

Journey to the Sorcerer

At ten that morning I heard a knock on the door. It was Zach, ready to take us to the ruins. I would be lying if I said I wasn't nervous. I had showered, and tried to dress as nicely as possible, in a button down black shirt and black pants. I pulled off black well, having black hair and all. I wore my new white glasses, which gave me more credibility than the black frames. I had already eaten a raw tuna steak for breakfast, a metaphor for my life. A fish from Alaska thousands of miles away swimming along minding its own business, when suddenly it is ripped out of the water. Taken from its natural environment it drowns in oxygen and is cut to pieces before being sent away. Then here I am taking it out of my freezer, thawing it and eating it's flesh. Was I the fisherman or the fish? Would I be able to avoid the net?

Afterward, I spent twenty minutes meditating at my altar. It was the not knowing that got to me. Everything was so mysterious about this Association. If it was anything like encountering their investigative team was, they should be the ones afraid of me, and the girl in my head, respectively. I hoped it wouldn't be that way. I imagined these were civil people. I mean, civil demons, anyway. How could I judge though? Maybe some of them were people too. There had to be exceptions. I said goodbye to Ezekiel, and swear he knew exactly what I was feeling. They say that animals have better emotional intuition than humans do.

The drive out to the ruins was as pretty as all New Mexico landscapes. When we were forty minutes into our trip, all of the other cars and civilization disappeared into empty mountainous landscapes. Places that were rarely seen by the human eye. It was like being an explorer. Discovering places no one knows exist. The last hour didn't even have a paved road. It was just a dirt path with no signs, I don't know how anyone found their way around here. Zach pulled into what was apparently a parking lot. There was even another car there!

"We have to walk the rest of the way," said Zach. I followed him out of the car and around the side of a mountain. It was impossible to tell how to get to the top. There were so many layers and levels that seemed to be the same one. You were never where you thought you would be when you got to the top of one. Finally we stopped on one of the ledges. I was out of breath from not having done this kind of thing in longer than I cared to admit. We were on a ledge with a stone wall behind us.

"There it is," Zach said, pointing to the flat wall.

"That rock?" I asked.

"We'll need to work on your demon vision when we get back," he said, putting his hands on the sides of my head and pointing my vision toward the wall. Slowly I could see the wall fade into a doorway. There was a secret entrance not visible to the naked eye. We walked through what looked like a solid wall of rock into a tunnel. At the end of the tunnel was a patch of ice that we both stood on. Zach spoke something in Latin, I don't know Latin well enough to write it out. Moments later we were sinking into the ice, though we didn't seem to be disturbing it at all. I was surprised I could still breath as I descended through this cold medium. I felt my legs dangling in open air and soon, as I continued through the ice, I dropped about six inches to the ground. Looking up, I saw nothing. Zach was standing there next to me. My clothes had gotten wet, but were not completely soaked through. I noticed it was raining here. Wherever here was. There wasn't much to see. It was another empty desert landscape with minimal shrubbery, mountains all around, and no signs of life.

"There it is," Zach said, pointing behind me. "The Association."

Turning around, I wondered how I missed this monolithic structure. It was a skyscraper in the middle of nowhere. I looked at my cell phone. No service. I wanted to snap a picture, but figured it wasn't a good idea. They might be watching. The sky was a medium-gray with no signs of sun, moon, or stars. I couldn't see clouds, but they must have been there. It was incredibly monotone, save for the beauty of the gentle rainfall. Rain is so beautiful. It is just like us. We rise up, we fall back down. Some of us become a river or a lake. Some are part of a moving stream, others a stationary puddle. We are consumed or evaporated and the cycle continues. It was very much like the life cycle that Zach spoke of. Energy in motion. There is so much we will never understand, and I can't even remember what I had for lunch yesterday. How macro does everything get, and how far away are we from it?

We approached the doors and heard a voice through a speaker above them.

"Identification please."

"3692, Zach, and 2517, Michael," Zach said.

"You are expected," the voice said. There was the sound of a sliding lock, and the doors opened to us. We walked through into a giant hall that looked like a fifteenth century mansion.

"Glad you could make it," said a tall thin man with grey hair and rectangular glasses. "My name is Lee. I'm the caretaker here." He had a good sense of style. His clothes were mostly dark, including platform shoes. He was wearing jewelry, but in a way that it meant nothing to him. Some people can pull it off. He had a weird way of moving his hand around as he talked that seemed like it was intended on building rapport. "Did you have a nice trip? Let's get you two some towels," he said, laughing with his full mouth, and shaking his head in an exaggerated laugh. I think it was supposed to put us at ease, though I could tell this man didn't care at all what we thought of him. We were wet from the rain and from traveling through the ice. "The directors are reviewing your case. They'll be ready to interview you in half an hour or so. Make yourselves comfortable by the fire. Would you like anything to drink?"

"Bottled water?" Zach asked.

"Yeah, we have that. It's Italian. Very good stuff. I'll bring it by in a minute, for you?" Lee said, pointing to me.

"Ginger beer?" I asked.

"No. No, we don't have that. What do you think this is? We might have ginger ale. Would you like that or how about a shot of whiskey?" He shook his head like I was crazy.

"Ginger ale is fine," I said. He walked away to get the drinks.

"You're going to have to be on your best behavior when we get up there," Zach said to me. "This is very serious." I nodded. The man came back with our drinks. I took a sip and realized that it was ginger ale, but also Irish whiskey. I swallowed it.

"Good huh? I thought you might like that," said Lee. He nodded his head and looked like he was going to say something else, but walked away instead. I wondered how long it had been since he had seen any new faces. Assuming they ever came down from the higher floors. There were probably living quarters in the building. Living quarters isn't a nice enough word for them. Probably more like penthouses. The view was great, but certainly vast and empty at the same time. This was an isolated place for the older beings to enjoy their lives in peace. About an hour later, Lee came back and told us it was time to go upstairs. He led us to the elevator and stayed outside while we went up to the top.

Chapter 30
Feeding the Cat
(From Jenny's perspective)

When I finally finished my bar shift, a bit before three, I remembered that I would have to go and check on Michael's cat. It was a bit irritating having to do favors, but he was always a good and happy person, so what was this small favor between friends? I pushed the buttons for the gate to open, and pulled around to visitor parking. The sun was burning bright, as always. At my age it was only a minor irritation, but still good not to stay out too long. This was a really nice place to live. Good location, good security, but I could never live somewhere without a yard, especially with my dog. I lifted the mat and unlocked the door. Looking in I could see Michael's cat, Ezekiel, sitting on top of the cat tower. I tried to take a step in, but something was stopping me. Why couldn't I enter? There was no one there.

Ezekiel jumped down from the cat tower and walked toward the middle of the room, looking at me the whole time. He licked a paw.

"I'm here to feed you, let me in," I said to him, as if he had any clue what I was talking about. "Ugh." Then he started to change. The little red cat mutated in size and shape until he became a man, almost as tall as me. This wasn't a cat after all.

"What, who are you?" I asked him.

"I am Ezekiel," said the man. "I am Michael's familiar. Why do you disgrace my doorstep with your presence, vampire?"

"Michael told me to come here and check on you, but clearly you're doing fine. I'm just going to go."

"Wait. Why would he have you come here to check on me?"

"I don't know. He said he was going to some petroglyphs and that he didn't know how long he would be gone and so he asked me to check on you."

"Did he say exactly where he went?"

"No, just that it was some ancient ruins a few hours away."

"Oh, no. The Association. We have to get him out of there."

"What? The Association? That thing is real? How could we possibly take them on? This is way more than I agreed to when I said I would check on you."

"Do you care about him at all? We have to do something," said Ezekiel.

Chapter 31
It's Just Like Waking Up

The elevator doors opened and there was a new escort on the top floor. He wasn't nearly as distinctive. Frankly, he was forgettable. The directors probably didn't want to compete for attention. Not that they would have to, but Lee was pretty attention-drawing.

The top floor looked similar to an ancient Roman wonder. There were giant stone pillars holding up the roof. There was nothing separating us from the outside world. The rain fell gently on the outer balcony, which didn't even have a railing. There were rows of booths, similar to a courtroom, facing an elevated platform where five men sat facing the crowd. These were the beings that legends were made after. We were led to the front row, and seated next to each other. Our belongings were laid out in front of us on a table that was just out of reach. They took my phone, my wallet, my bracelet, and my cross.

"Very nice," said one of them. They had all been looking at my bracelet. Coveting it. Feeling it's power. I objected to the removal of my cross, but figured if I was going to go demon, this would be an okay place for it.

The man in the middle seemed to be the leader of the group. He stood up and addressed me.

"First, I would like to take a moment to apologize to you for a few things," he said. "The men that we sent to investigate were acting on their own accord when they tried to interrogate you and we do not condone their actions. That being said, their deaths are not on your hands. They were humans who made a mistake, and got what they had coming to them. Therefore, that part is being dismissed from evidence. Second, we are aware that you acted unknowingly during most of these events. Your true nature was kept from you for most of your life, and we understand that it led to most of these incidents. Zach, as your watcher, should have been able to see it sooner, but we understand why it was overlooked."

"Do I get a chance to explain?" I asked.

The man on the right side of the directors stood up and yelled at me, "You will speak when spoken to," he said. The leading director in the middle held up his hand toward the other director, presumably in a higher position. The other man sat back down.

"We already know everything. You don't get to live this long without a few tricks up your sleeves. You are not here to be put on trial. We are much past that point. You are here to be sentenced." I felt a weight inside of me. I wouldn't be able to do anything to defend myself. "Now then. You are not off the hook for killing your demon brethren. You may remember from the black SUV incident. He was acting beyond his means, but you did not have our consent for termination. This is a violation of our codes of conduct. On top of that, you made your presence known to a lower species, compromising our very presence here on earth. That is much more serious. We are aware that you have no demon training, whatsoever, and that is part of the reason we didn't just have you killed. Before we come to a final conclusion, we are going to tell you what we are considering. It is obvious to us that you are an unsuitable candidate for reinsertion into society at this point in time. That being said, we do not believe that we need to terminate your existence either. The most likely course of action is that you will be kept here with us for a minimum of one hundred years for proper education and training. We consider it an experiment that failed, having you live in society as a normal person without teaching you what was right and wrong. Part of the blame for that lies with us. The rest with you and your watcher, Zach. After the time period has elapsed, you will no longer be known to anyone living, and we can build a new life for you, assuming that all went well during your educational period. We are going to vote on whether or not this will be the course of action we will take at this point. Know that we consider it fair and just and that our decision will be final."

They were going to take away my life. Everything. Everyone I knew and loved. Everyone I hated. Everything I thought was mine. My home, my books, my cat. My family. It would all be gone. I would be an outsider, thrown into a new society. After having to live here with them for a century. They didn't have my permission to take away my life. That was my choice to make. Freedom was such a diluted concept. I can carry on in some other way. I stood up and walked to the table.

"Stop him!" yelled the man on the far end of the panel.

"I must insist that you take your seat," said the Leader. I picked up the bracelet and put in on. The guard ran over to stop me, but I already felt it's power. I waved my arm at him, and he was thrown backward into the elevator doors.

"Stop this immediately!" said the Leader. They were all standing at this point. I think they were planning on coming down after me. I picked up the cross and looked at it, then closed my hand and held onto it tightly. Zach stood up, supporting my decision. He threw over the table, and pulled out a piece of chalk he had been hiding in a secret pocket of his pants. He started drawing and scribbling on the ground with it.

"Go," he said to me. "I will see you next time." I nodded back to him and walked out to the edge of the balcony. I looked up to the sky to feel the raindrops falling on my face one last time. I turned around, the heels of my feet already over the edge.

"Get back here!" demanded the leader. The ground was shaking, something was happening from the symbols Zach was drawing. The building was coming down. I took a deep breath and released it. Take me away. They were only a few feet away, when I fell backwards off of the balcony. It was a long way down. As I was falling, there was a brief moment when the raindrops fell at the same speed as I did. It was like everything had frozen. Beautiful. Most people die from a heart attack before hitting the ground, knowing that their death is coming. Not me. I couldn't have been more relaxed. This whole experience had been one giant ball of suffering. It was time for release. It was too fast to even feel it.

My cross lay a few feet from my body. The glow of the bracelet faded. A few feet away, Jenny was walking toward my body. I don't know if it really was her, or the last projection of a dying brain, adding to my suffering. She kneeled down next to me and gently rubbed my face with the back of her hand. Jenny leaned in closer and gave me a gentle kiss on the cheek, then moved downward toward my throat. My hand twitched.